I KEPT PRESSING THE **100** MILLION-YEAR **BUTTON** AND CAME OUT ON TOP
~THE UNBEATABLE REJECT SWORDSMAN~

5

"What was that? Don't get carried away, 'Wonder Girl,' or whatever the hell your nickname is."

Shido

A first year at Ice King Academy, one of the Elite Five Academies. Boasts overwhelming talent with the sword. Goes to White Lily to take Allen for himself.

"Allen is
mine now.
I won't
give him
to you."

Idora Luksmaria

A first year at White Lily Girls
Academy, one of the Elite Five
Academies. She is a prodigy who
people have dubbed the "Wonder
Child." Takes advantage of Allen's
temporary transfer to White Lily
to try and get closer to him.

"What do you mean?"

Lia Vesteria

Princess of Vesteria Kingdom and Allen's roommate. She is recommended to become a senior holy knight special trainee alongside Allen.

Rose Valencia

The sole inheritor of the Cherry Blossom Blade School of Swordcraft. She is recommended to become a senior holy knight special trainee alongside Allen.

"Anyway, I have a proposal for you all...

Would you be interested in a foreign expedition?"

Clown Jester

The new branch manager of the Holy Knights Association's Aurest branch. An enigmatic man with a lighthearted, slippery demeanor.

In that tense atmosphere, Allen finally unleashed his long-coveted power. The true ebon sword appeared through a rift in the air. Its blade, hilt, and guard were all pitch-black. It was Allen's Soul Attire, the ultimate sword he had struggled so desperately to obtain.

"Destroy– Insatiable Demon Zeon!"

Raine Grad

One of the Black Organization's Thirteen Oracle Knights. Conquered Daglio, the Land of Sunshine, with his overwhelming strength.

CONTENTS

I KEPT PRESSING THE 100-MILLION-YEAR BUTTON AND CAME OUT ON TOP

~THE UNBEATABLE REJECT SWORDSMAN~

5

SYUICHI TSUKISHIMA

Illustration by **MOKYU**

YEN ON

New York

I KEPT PRESSING THE 100-MILLION-YEAR BUTTON AND CAME OUT
ON TOP: ~THE UNBEATABLE REJECT SWORDSMAN~
SYUICHI TSUKISHIMA

Translation by Luke Hutton
Cover art by Mokyu

1 OKUNEN BUTTON WO RENDA SHITA ORE HA, KIZUITARA SAIKYO NI
NATTE ITA Vol.5 ~RAKUDAI KENSHI NO GAKUIN MUSO~
©Syuichi Tsukishima, Mokyu 2020
First published in Japan in 2020 by KADOKAWA CORPORATION, Tokyo.
English translation rights arranged with KADOKAWA CORPORATION, Tokyo,
through TUTTLE-MORI AGENCY, INC., Tokyo

Yen On
150 West 30th Street, 19th Floor
New York, NY 10001

Visit us at yenpress.com
facebook.com/yenpress
twitter.com/yenpress
yenpress.tumblr.com
instagram.com/yenpress

First Yen On Edition: May 2023
Edited by Yen On Editorial: Maya Deutsch
Designed by Yen Press Design: Andy Swist

Yen On is an imprint of Yen Press, LLC.
The Yen On name and logo are trademarks of Yen Press, LLC.

Library of Congress Cataloging-in-Publication Data
Names: Tsukishima, Syuichi, author. | Mokyu, illustrator. | Hutton, Luke, translator.
Title: I kept pressing the 100-million-year button and came out on top /
Syuichi Tsukishima ; illustration by Mokyu ; translation by Luke Hutton.
Other titles: Ichiokunen button o renda shita ore wa, kizuitara saikyo ni natte ita. English
Description: First Yen On edition. | New York, NY : Yen On, 2021–
Identifiers: LCCN 2021034588 | ISBN 9781975322342 (v. 1 ; trade paperback) |
ISBN 9781975322366 (v. 2 ; trade paperback) | ISBN 9781975322380
(v. 3 ; trade paperback) | ISBN 9781975343163 (v. 4 ; trade paperback) |
ISBN 9781975343187 (v. 5 ; trade paperback)
Subjects: LCGFT: Fantasy fiction. | Light novels.
Classification: LCC PL876.S857 I3413 2021 | DDC 895.6/36—dc23
LC record available at https://lccn.loc.gov/2021034588

ISBNs: 978-1-9753-4318-7 (paperback)
978-1-9753-4319-4 (ebook)

10 9 8 7 6 5 4 3 2 1

LSC-C

Printed in the United States of America

CHAPTER 1

Strange Times at White Lily Girls Academy

"What the heck happened here?!" I asked aloud. Thousand Blade Academy had been completely destroyed. I stood there in dumbfounded silence as I took in the unbelievable sight.

"Allen?! Is that you, Allen?!"

Chairwoman Reia dashed out of a charred school building. She was wearing her usual black suit, along with a yellow helmet that read SAFETY FIRST.

"Chairwoman Reia!" I exclaimed.

"It's so great to see you safe and sound! I was right to stick around here on the off chance you showed up!" the chairwoman said, smiling with relief and patting me on the back.

"Um, what's going on here?" I asked.

"Hmm… Let's go inside. I'll tell you all about it in my office," she answered, glancing toward the beaten-up main school building.

"I-is it really safe to go in there?" It appeared as though it could collapse at any moment…

"Totally. The main building has a strong foundation. It looks like it's in horrible condition, but there's no actual danger of it collapsing. Plus, we don't know who could be listening in on our conversation out here."

"I-I see." I was a bit worried, but if anything happened, I could just cloak myself in darkness.

"All right, let's go inside," the chairwoman said.

"Yes, ma'am," I responded.

I followed Chairwoman Reia and stepped into the ruins of Thousand Blade's campus.

■

Rubble was strewn throughout the hallways of the main school building, making it difficult to walk. The interior had proved more stable than I expected, though—the foundation must truly have been sturdy.

I decided to ask the chairwoman about something on the way to her office. "Um, how are Lia and Rose?"

"Ah, yes. They were both admitted to a nearby hospital," she answered.

"Oh no! Are they okay?!"

"Don't worry, they're only receiving an examination to be safe. I went to see them this morning, and they were both in tip-top shape. They were dying to dash out of there and start looking for you."

"Okay. That's good to hear." Relief washed over me as we arrived at the chair's office.

"Go ahead," Chairwoman Reia said, ushering me in.

"Thank you," I answered, stepping inside. She sat in her chair and faced me from the other side of her desk.

"All right, I'm going to tell you about what happened yesterday... But first, how much do you remember?" she asked.

"...!" She somehow knew that parts of my memory were missing. That was going to save a lot of time. "I can recall everything until the moment Dodriel stabbed me through the heart. What happened after that is mostly blank. Next thing I knew, I came to in a forest."

"Hmm, I see... I have a pretty good idea of what you experienced. Let's talk about what happened after you lost consciousness."

"Please."

The chairwoman then revealed the shocking truth. She told me that the wicked Spirit Core inside me had gone berserk and trounced Dodriel and Fuu. His strength was so overwhelming that he'd cut down one hundred members of the Black Organization on top of that, laying waste to the academy in the process. This was way too much for me to take in at once.

"Did my Spirit Core...really do all that?" I asked weakly.

"Yes. Every word I've said is true." She nodded solemnly, and a heavy silence befell us.

"I'm sorry... It sounds like I've caused you a lot of trouble...," I said, beginning to lower my head in apology. The chairwoman quickly stopped me.

"Hey now, don't get the wrong idea. You did us a great service. I can think of all kinds of horrible things that could have happened if you hadn't been there," she objected.

"What do you mean?"

"The entire student body could have gotten killed, Lia could have been kidnapped, the Black Organization could have escaped...and so on," she muttered with a bitter expression, and continued speaking. "If any of that had come to pass, Thousand Blade would have shut down, and the country would have fallen into chaos. It's entirely thanks to you that everyone is safe. I am truly grateful."

The chairwoman stood up and bowed deeply.

"P-please stop that! I didn't do anything worthy of that kind of praise! It was all *him*—my Spirit Core!" I protested.

"Cease the humility. The deputy chairman told me you destroyed an extremely sophisticated barrier for us. And besides, the strength of a Spirit Core reflects the strength of its swordsman. You should be proud. It was your strength alone that saved the academy."

"O-okay..."

No matter what Reia said, it still didn't feel like I had done anything to save the academy, rather than harm it. I sat there confused, and the chairwoman stared at me in silence.

First he regenerates at shocking speed, and now his Spirit Core's white hair is mixing into his own... This is bad. The path is opening significantly faster than I expected. At this rate, it won't be long before...

Her expression rapidly grew grim.

"Chairwoman... Is something wrong?"

"No, I was just thinking. Don't worry about it."

"Okay... You must be working really hard." She'd been summoned by the government, only for the Black Organization to immediately attack her academy—she must have been exhausted.

"No, that's not it. I'm making full use of Eighteen, so I'm not that tired. That being said, there's one more thing I should touch on— the people who were arrested." The chairwoman cleared her throat and began to read the summary of a report from the holy knights. "We captured about three hundred and fifty members of the Black Organization. Unfortunately, Fuu Ludoras and Dodriel Barton appear to have escaped. Dodriel may have used his shadow powers to teleport himself and Fuu away... What an annoying ability," she muttered, perturbed.

"Huh? Do you know who Dodriel is, Chairwoman?" I asked.

"Of course. He's a rising star in the Black Organization who's been causing trouble all across the continent recently. He's extremely tough and can apparently recover from any lethal wound. Most worrisome is that strange Soul Attire of his, which can control shadows... It renders border security completely ineffectual. The Black Organization members who attacked the academy were likely sent here using his shadow powers."

"Really..." I hadn't realized Dodriel had become such an infamous criminal.

"I suppose that's all I have to tell you. Is there anything else that's bothering you?" she asked, giving me a chance to ask some questions.

I have to ask this, don't I? It was an extremely difficult question. *But I can't allow myself to run away from this.* I may have been unconscious, but that didn't change the fact that my body had done these deeds. I couldn't avert my gaze from the lives I'd taken.

"Um, Chairwoman... Of the people *he* cut down, how many died?" I asked after steeling myself.

"Zero. Not a single person succumbed to their wounds," she answered. I couldn't believe my ears.

"S-seriously?!"

"Yep. They were all heavily injured and barely clinging to life, but not a single death has been confirmed."

"But why would he leave them alive?"

My Spirit Core was extremely violent. The last time he'd emerged in the real world—at the Elite Five Holy Festival—he attempted to kill Shido without hesitation. I would have expected him to slaughter to his heart's content without anyone there to stop him.

"That was probably intentional on his part," the chairwoman answered.

"Intentional? What do you mean?" I asked.

"You have an aversion to killing, don't you?"

"O-of course I do!" He and I were nothing alike. I wasn't some battle-crazed maniac who took pleasure in blood and violence.

"I'm only grasping at straws here, but...he was probably trying to avoid stimulating your consciousness. Since he's your Spirit Core, you have the capacity to greatly limit his activities. Doing something as shocking as murder would have roused you from slumber. He wouldn't have been able to remain in the surface world for long after that. I assume that's why he went out of his way to avoid killing anyone."

"That makes sense..." That reminded me of something similar he'd said in the Soul World once, about it being difficult to hijack my body while I was conscious.

"There's one thing we can be sure of—he achieved *something* while he was in control of your body. There's no way he would have returned it so easily otherwise," she declared.

"What did he do?" I asked.

"Unfortunately, I don't know the answer to that. But I have no doubt it was nothing good."

"...That's for sure."

Our conversation reached a pause, and the chairwoman clapped her hands.

"Okay, well, that's enough about the past. Let's talk about what's next in store. As you can see, Thousand Blade cannot serve as an effective swordcraft academy in this state. There's no way we can hold classes."

While the building wasn't going to collapse anytime soon, she was definitely right that it would be impossible to learn here.

"Reconstruction of the main building is set to begin this afternoon. It'll be a large-scale operation utilizing self-strengthening and remote-control Soul Attire. I expect the academy will be back to normal in two weeks."

"Only two weeks?!"

"Hmm-hmm-hmm, that's scary fast, isn't it? It's going to cost a fortune, though..." Reia paled and stared out the window. "Anyway, that means Thousand Blade Academy will be closed for two weeks starting tomorrow, but I can't afford for you students to take all the time off. True swordfighters need to train hard every day."

She nodded and continued.

"That's why you all will take special classes at Ice King Academy until Thousand Blade's reconstruction is complete."

"That's Shido's school." I was fine with that. Ice King Academy was another of the Elite Five Academies. Training on a daily basis with Shido sounded like the best thing I could ask for.

"Yes. This will be quite the stimulating experience for both academies! But I have something a little different planned for *you*, Allen," she said suggestively.

"What's that?"

"Unlike everyone else, I am sending you to White Lily Girls Academy. You remember that school, right? It's one of the Elite Five Academies. Idora Luksmaria, the 'Wonder Child' you defeated in the Sword Master Festival, goes there."

"What?! You're joking, right?! That's a girls' academy!"

"It *is* an all-female school, yes—but that won't be a problem."

I couldn't imagine how a male student transferring to a girls' academy *wouldn't* be a problem.

"This isn't known to the public yet, but White Lily is planning on going co-ed a few years from now. You can consider yourself the first trial run ahead of their goal."

"H-huh…" This was the first I'd heard of that. "But am I really the best choice for the first test case? That sounds really important. Honestly, I think there are other guys better suited to this."

"Ha, what are you saying? You're the most qualified person in existence. You're an alien when it comes to repressing your sexual desires. I can send you to White Lily worry-free," Chairwoman Reia insisted.

"…An alien?" I repeated, tilting my head in confusion. I didn't know what she meant.

"You're living under the same roof with Lia Vesteria—a stunningly hot babe—and you even have a master-slave relationship with her, yet you haven't had one incident. Who *wouldn't* think you're from another planet?"

"I-incident…? Of course there hasn't been an incident!" I protested, cheeks flushing.

"Ha-ha-ha, take that as a joke if you wish. Still, the students at White Lily are all fine ladies, and they're almost entirely unaccustomed to men. That makes a guy with a gentle disposition like you the perfect guinea pig. Also, I hear Idora really hopes that you'll transfer. Their chairwoman is very enthusiastic about your arrival, too."

"Idora wants me there?"

"Yeah. She seems quite infatuated with you. I've heard she's been collecting recordings of all your matches in the Sword Master Festival to study in her free time. She has a burning desire for vengeance."

"Ah-ha-ha, that's pretty scary…" It sounded like our next duel was going to be even more intense.

"Anyway, that's why you're being sent to White Lily Girls Academy. If you really don't want to go, though, I can tell their chairwoman that you aren't interested. In that case you'll go to Ice King Academy with everyone else. So what'll it be?" she asked.

In other words, I wasn't being forced to go there. "That's a difficult question…"

I could go to White Lily on my own, or attend Ice King with all my classmates. *The prospect of training with Shido sounds incredibly appealing, but I don't know if I'll get a chance to practice with Idora ever again.* The problem was that White Lily was an all-girls school. Thousand Blade and Ice King were both co-ed, so White Lily might be a difficult adjustment. *I don't know what to do…*

I fretted over the decision, and the chairwoman spoke up.

"To be totally honest with you, Thousand Blade could really stand to benefit from you going to White Lily. It's a renowned powerhouse of an academy. If we can form a pipeline with them, we'll be able to raise the level of our students through more student exchange," she admitted. "Beyond that, living at White Lily will be invigorating. The culture is just as competitive as at Thousand Blade, if not more so. The students are always lifting one another to greater heights. The Skills Challenge they hold every month has a reputation for getting very heated. The environment, the friends you'll make, and the classes you'll take will differ dramatically from Thousand Blade and Ice King, which should help you grow immensely."

"That does sound nice…," I responded.

Idora was far from the only skilled swordswoman at White Lily. There were also the two girls who'd defeated Lilim and Tirith in the Royal

Sword Festival. Their captain, Lily Gonzales, was also incredibly intimidating despite her loss to Sebas. There was a lot I could learn from them.

"Okay. This sounds like too good of an opportunity to pass up, so I'll go to White Lily Girls Academy," I said.

"Awesome! I'll contact their chairwoman. Give this pamphlet a quick look-through by tomorrow," she responded, handing me a White Lily new student guidebook.

"Yes, ma'am."

And that was how I ended up attending White Lily Girls Academy, Idora Luksmaria's school, for a brief two-week period.

■

The next day, I found myself standing in front of the main entrance to White Lily Girls Academy. Lia and Rose were with me.

"That's a really extravagant structure...," I remarked.

White Lily's main school building towered before us. It looked as grand and beautiful as an ivory palace.

"It's just as pretty as they say," Lia observed.

"Yeah. It's really awe-inspiring," Rose agreed.

They both sighed in admiration.

I can't believe they both decided to come with me... After speaking with Chairwoman Reia yesterday, I'd visited the hospital where Lia and Rose were being examined. They were so relieved to see I was okay that they didn't immediately notice that some of my hair had gone white. They were surprised by the sudden color change, but unexpectedly, they both liked it.

I mentioned my transfer to White Lily once our conversation slowed down, and their reaction was dramatic. They both declared, ""I can't let you go alone to that girls-only school!"" and rushed to meet with Chairwoman Reia. The pair wrestled permission from her to join me after a little negotiation, and here we were.

The area around us suddenly grew noisy as we looked up at the building.

"What is that gentleman doing at this academy?"

"Is that Allen Rodol? The one who defeated Big Sis?"

"What ever are students from Thousand Blade doing here?"

Evidently, we were quite conspicuous dressed in our Thousand Blade uniforms.

"Lia, Rose, let's go ahead and meet with the chairwoman," I suggested.

"Yeah, let's go," Lia responded.

"Roger that," Rose said.

We walked through the gate, entered the main school building, and encountered a familiar face.

"Greetings. Thank you for coming, Allen. And…you two are Lia and Rose, correct? Welcome to White Lily," she said.

It was Idora Luksmaria. Her beautiful white hair was done in a half-up style. She was tall for a fifteen-year-old girl and stood at about 165 centimeters in height. Her eyes were a clear amber, her skin was white as snow, and her limbs were long and slender—she was a girl of truly unmatched beauty. Wearing the green and white dress that served as the White Lily uniform, she welcomed us warmly with a smile.

"Good morning, Idora," I responded.

"I'm Lia Vesteria. It's a pleasure to meet you. We'll only be here for a short while, but I hope we can get along," Lia said politely.

"I'm Rose Valencia. Nice to meet you," Rose added.

It took a second for Idora to respond.

"…Oh, I'm Idora Luksmaria. Nice to meet you, too." Her self-introduction had come a little late; she always seemed to be off in her own little world. "Come. I'll show you around," she told us, beginning to walk down the hallway.

"I appreciate the thought, but we're supposed to meet with the chairwoman first…," I informed her.

"It's fine. The chairwoman asked me to do this. That waste-of-oxygen never arrives at the academy before noon," Idora explained.

"Oh, really?"

"Yeah. She's little more than decoration."

"I see…"

It sounded like White Lily's chairwoman did just as little work as ours.

"I'll guide you instead," Idora said.

"That would be great," I responded.

Idora then began our tour of White Lily Girls Academy. The grounds were expansive, and the school had a rich supply of training equipment, including a shockingly large amount of soul-crystal swords and training blades. *White Lily's facilities are just as high-end as Thousand Blade's. They might even be better.* It wasn't one of the Elite Five Academies for nothing.

I had been a little worried about the bathrooms and locker rooms, but I was relieved to hear I would be able to use the facilities for the male professors. So far, it was looking like my student life wouldn't lack for anything.

"That's about it for the main building… Was that helpful?" Idora asked with an adorable tilt of her head after guiding us through the building's three floors.

"Yes, it was. Thank you very much, Idora," I responded.

"Good. Okay, the gym and the art building are up next," she said.

We followed after her as she left the main school building. Just as we walked through the entrance to the gymnasium, I heard a commotion at the gate to the academy.

"*Tch*… Get the hell out of my way! I'll kill you!"

"Stand down and let us through if you do not want to receive divine punishment!"

I heard two male voices shouting violently.

"C-calm down, you two!"

"As I said… We can't let you through without an entry permit!"

I also heard two guards trying to deescalate things. We were a good distance away from the gate, but their exchange was so heated that I could hear every word they were saying.

"Goddamn pricks… I TOLD YOU TO MOVE!"

"GAH!"

The guards screamed as they were sent flying through the air. A terrible possibility occurred to me.

"…Oh no. Is it the Black Organization again?!" I shouted. Their failed attempt to abduct Lia had taken place only a few days ago. It wouldn't be surprising if they were already trying again.

"Let's go, Allen!" urged Lia.

"We'll send them packing this time!" Rose declared.

They had both already drawn their swords—it looked like they were thinking the same thing.

"Yeah!" I responded.

"I'm coming, too!" Idora said.

She and I nodded at each other, and we all immediately dashed for the gate. I was in for a shock when we arrived.

"You all have guts for stealing Allen from us… Where is he?!"

"Return our Lord Allen to us! Capturing God is an unforgivable sin! Just who do you all think you are?!"

The two people yelling were none other than Shido Jukurius and Cain Material, first years from Ice King Academy.

"Sh-Shido?! Cain?!" I shouted, widening my eyes with surprise at the identities of the violent offenders.

"You bastard… So this is where you've been hiding, Allen! Kiss this boring dump goodbye and come with us!" Shido commanded after he noticed me.

"I am so glad to see that you're safe, my lord! Let us return to Ice King Academy!" Cain said.

I couldn't believe my ears. The guards stared pointedly at me, demanding I get these apparent acquaintances of mine under control.

"U-umm...," I stammered, unsure of what to say. Idora stood in front of me.

"Allen is mine now. I won't give him to you," she declared.

"What was that? Don't get carried away 'Wonder Girl,' or whatever the hell your nickname is," Shido responded, furrowing his eyebrows threateningly.

"H-he's yours, you say?! God belongs to everyone! Your blasphemy goes too far, Idora Luksmaria!" Cain yelled. I didn't have any idea what he meant.

This is getting bad, I thought, immediately stepping into the middle of their spat. "L-let's just calm down! Can't we talk about this without resorting to violence?" I pleaded.

Idora and Shido both glanced at me before facing each other again.

"Hand him over," Shido demanded.

"No," Idora rejected.

Shido and Idora's attempt to negotiate collapsed in all of two seconds. Their communication skills were both lacking, so there hadn't been much of a chance they would manage a decent conversation. *Shido is about to blow his top, and Idora isn't the type to mince words... Damn it, what should I do...?* I'd fumbled for a way to get a hold of this situation, only to watch it spiral further out of control.

"Consume—Ice Wolf Vanargand!"

"Fulfill—Neba Grome!"

Shido and Idora summoned their Soul Attires at the exact same time. Frigid air and blue lightning burst forth from their swords, and sparks flew from their fierce gazes.

Crap, this is getting really bad! They could level White Lily if they fought here. Shido had always had a short temper, but I hadn't expected Idora to also go this far.

"I'll kill you...," Shido seethed.

"Go ahead and try!" Idora fired back.

Their incompatible personalities escalated the situation, fanning the flames of their tempers even hotter. There was no way they were going to calm down on their own.

"Oh, come on… Lay off already!" I pleaded in a firm tone. In that instant, I enveloped the entirety of White Lily in pitch-black darkness.

"What the… When did you get this powerful?!" Shido shouted.

"Allen, just how strong are you?!" Idora asked.

They both stared at me in shock through the gloom.

"H-huh?" I repressed the powerful darkness flooding out of my body. "A-anyway… Can we talk about this without getting violent?" I said, reiterating my request.

"What in the world was that wicked darkness?!"

A moment later, a small girl rushed toward us from outside the main gate. Upon closer inspection, I realized that she had a fittingly small sword at her hip that looked like a *wakizashi*, a short katana. She was probably a student at a middle school swordcraft academy.

"Umm… Are you at the wrong academy? This is a high school," I informed her.

"D-don't treat me like a child! I am Kemmi Fasta, the chairwoman of White Lily Girls Academy!" she responded with an offended expression, flashing a staff ID at me that read WHITE LILY GIRLS ACADEMY CHAIRWOMAN KEMMI FASTA.

"Wh-what?!" I exclaimed, staring at Kemmi in wide-eyed disbelief.

Kemmi Fasta had frizzy black hair that reached her back. She stood at about 140 centimeters tall. Her complexion was so youthful, she would never be able to buy alcohol without getting carded, and she was wearing a coat that was entirely too big for her. There was no world in which she didn't look like a child.

This time I was in the wrong. Ms. Paula always told me it was "disrespectful to treat a grown woman like a child."

"…Sorry, that was very rude of me," I apologized.

"Hmph. As long as you understand," she said, folding her arms. Her every action looked childish. I couldn't help but worry about her.

"Hey, short stuff. You the chairwoman of this dump?" Shido asked rudely.

"Y-you're that delinquent, Shido... For what purpose do you grace this academy, fine sir?" Kemmi responded, hiding behind Idora and while using bizarrely polite language. She was clearly intimidated by Shido's glare. She must have struggled with rough personalities like him.

"I'll give it to you straight: Hand over Allen," he demanded curtly.

"U-umm, well... My apologies, but I am not sure that is a request I can fulfill. I made a promise to Thousand Blade Academy...," Kemmi responded as politely as possible, still looking timid.

"Fine, then I'll transfer here," Shido declared.

"Th-that is a difficult request to meet as well. This is an academy for maidens, you see... A dangerou—er, *slightly unruly* gentleman such as yourself may not be the best fit...," the chairwoman squeaked, refusing Shido's second demand.

"Tch, it's just like Madam said..." Shido clicked his tongue loudly and produced an elegant envelope out of a pocket. "This is for you. Our chairwoman gave it to me."

"This is from Ferris...?" Kemmi fearfully accepted the envelope, which had an eastern design, and read the letter inside. "Hmm... Wait, how does she...?! Oh, interesting..." Her expression shifted rapidly as she read the letter. "Okay, I understand the situation. Shido, Cain, I grant you both permission to transfer here for a period of two weeks."

I had no idea what had caused her to change her mind, but she readily approved their transfer.

"Hell yeah!" Shido shouted.

"Wow! You did it, Shido!" Cain celebrated.

"...Chairwoman Kemmi?" Idora said, glaring daggers at the small woman as Shido and Cain shouted with joy.

"Wh-what is it, Idora?" Kemmi responded.

"What did that letter say?" Idora inquired.

"U-uh, well… It was a very nice missive! It was so touching that I couldn't help but approve their transfer!" Kemmi exclaimed shrilly, avoiding Idora's gaze. She was acting very suspiciously.

"Are you lying?" Idora asked. She stared at the chairwoman and took one step toward her.

"What, do you not believe your chairwoman?!"

"No, I don't."

"?!"

Kemmi went speechless at Idora's immediate reply.

"Look me straight in the eyes. Can you say definitively that you have nothing to feel guilty about?" Idora insisted.

"Um… Well…," Kemmi stammered, turning evasive.

"I knew it. You're hiding something, aren't you?" Idora accused.

"No, I'm not! I swear I'm not!" Kemmi shouted, growing flustered. The letter in question fell out of her pocket. Not allowing the chance to go to waste, Idora quickly snatched it off the ground. "Huh?! I-Idora! Respect your teacher's privacy!"

Ignoring Kemmi's protests, Idora casually read the letter aloud.

> Dear Kemmi,
>
> My Shido said he wants to spend time with Allen, so I'm giving him permission to go to White Lily. I'm not asking you to accept him for free, of course. I heard you took out an enormous loan from Fox Financing last month after incurring significant gambling losses. How about I take over that debt for you? That sounds appealing, no? All you have to do is look after my adorable Shido…and that idiot Cain as well. I entrust them to your care.
>
> Sincerely,
> Ferris Dorhein

The atmosphere grew tense after Kemmi's crooked deal was exposed. It sounded like she was a bit of a…no, a *very* problematic person.

"I-I'm so sorry…," Kemmi apologized pitifully, unable to take everyone's stares, and she bowed. "I know it is wrong of me as a teacher to accept shady deals like this. But my loan from Fox Financing is truly enormous… I'm never going to be able to repay it with my salary alone. Kids like you cannot possibly understand how hard it is to save money!"

"If you know how hard it is to save money, you never should've gambled to the point where you needed to take out a loan in the first place," Idora scolded.

"Ah…" Her sound argument pierced Kemmi's chest like a blade. "A-anyway, this is a huge opportunity for me… All I have to do is approve their transfer, and the debt will disappear!"

White Lily's chairwoman seemed very immature for her age. She stared Idora directly in the eyes.

"I swear I'll never gamble again! I'll even give up alcohol, too! Probably! So please…please just let me have this,…," she pleaded, prostrating herself on the ground. She desperately wanted to take this deal.

"Y-you don't have to go that far!" I quickly said to stop her, but Idora signaled for me to be quiet.

"Chairwoman. How many times have you kneeled before me like you are now?" Idora asked with exasperation.

"Grk…" It sounded like Kemmi gave out these dramatic apologies pretty often.

"That reminds me… A number of the student submissions at this year's White Lily Art Festival went missing. I heard later that they ended up being sold on the black market… You were responsible for that, weren't you?" Idora accused.

"Ha-ha-ha… Oh come on. I'm the chairwoman, I would never do something so unscrupulous…," Kemmi responded, slowly raising her head and forcing a smile.

"Is that the truth? Can you definitively say that you didn't do it?" Idora pressed.

"Wh-where's your proof…? If you doubt me that much, you should have evidence!" the chairwoman shouted at Idora angrily. She was only making herself look guiltier.

"Yes, of course," Idora said, pulling a picture out of her uniform pocket. It clearly showed Kemmi selling a beautiful painting.

"Eeee?!"

Kemmi gave an inhuman screech and tore the picture to pieces.

"That's a duplicate. I have the original safely stored in a different location," Idora informed her.

"Gack?!" Despite being at Idora's mercy, Kemmi smiled boldly. "H-how naive of you! All works in the Art Festival become the property of White Lily Girls Academy upon submission! And all things belonging to the academy belong to the chairwoman! It is my right to dispose of my property however I wish!"

"Will the board of directors and the parents association agree with that sentiment?"

"U-uhhh…"

"You also made a huge fuss about some of the admissions fees being stolen… You didn't embezzle that money, did you? That is undeniably a crime."

"…" Kemmi froze up completely after Idora's third accusation. Her closet was brimming with skeletons. "I am so sorry. This is all clearly due to my own moral shortcomings. I have no words to defend myself…"

Her forehead brushed the ground once again. She displayed none of the dignity you would expect of an academy chair as she threw herself down before us. The other students passing by pretending they didn't see anything; they, too, must have been sick of watching Kemmi grovel.

"Haah… Despite everything, you're still our chairwoman at the end of the day. I'll leave the final call to you," Idora said.

"Hooray! Welcome to White Lily Girls Academy, Shido and Cain!" Kemmi rejoiced, quickly jumping to her feet.

A-amazing. She's not showing an ounce of remorse... I could see why Idora and the other White Lily students were fed up with her.

"Oh, the bell is about to ring. New transfers, you are all in classroom 1-A. I am the homeroom teacher, so you can ask me anything!" she informed us. She walked to the main school building with a spring in her step, thrilled at the prospect of being unburdened of debt.

■

We were given a little bit of time in homeroom to perform quick self-introductions. Lia and Rose looked like they would have no trouble adjusting to the all-female class, and Cain was also given a warm welcome, thanks to his relatively relaxed demeanor.

Everyone's a little scared of Shido and me, though... My new classmates were afraid of me on account of my black and white hair, and Shido because of his menacing face, foul language, and bad attitude. It would likely take some time for us to break the ice.

Kemmi clapped her hands, snapping my thoughts back to the present. "First period is Soul Attire class. Grab a towel and a water bottle and follow me to the Soul Attire Room," she announced.

We all followed her to the underground Soul Attire Room. It looked like Soul Attire classes here weren't too different from those at Thousand Blade. Kemmi instructed us to grab a soul-crystal sword and face our Spirit Core—the same method used at my school.

"All right, begin whenever you are ready," Kemmi instructed.

Upon her order, all of my classmates closed their eyes and began to sink into the Soul World. I followed their examples and readied my soul-crystal sword at my chest. *Oh yeah, I haven't spoken to him in a while...,* I thought as my consciousness sank deeper and deeper into the depths of my soul.

Next thing I knew, I found myself in a sprawling wasteland. I looked up at a cracked boulder and saw *him* sitting atop it like he always.

"Good lord, you never learn… How the hell do you not realize how weak you are compared to me? Do you have rocks for brains?" he admonished.

"I guess so," I responded, brushing aside his abusive language. I then bowed. "Thank you. You saved us."

"…Huh?" He scowled in confusion. He had no idea why I was thanking him.

"I'm talking about what you did a few days ago. If you hadn't cut down those assailants, Lia would certainly have been kidnapped by the Black Organization. Rose and Shii probably would have been killed. So thank you."

My Spirit Core was a wicked being who took pleasure in blood and violence, but that was beside the point. He'd saved my friends and me, so I needed to thank him for that.

"God, you give me the creeps… Why don't you just get back to your pointless practice swings!" he shouted, visibly offended, before he entered striking range with only a single step. "*Hraagh!*" He swung at me with a straight right hand that surpassed the speed of sound. I ducked to evade it.

"Huh?!" he gasped. His eyes were wide with astonishment—he'd never expected me to dodge that for a second.

"I've gotten a little stronger, too," I said. I covered my sheathed blade in darkness and produced a mock black sword. "Seventh Style—Draw Flash!" I performed my quickest draw strike in my arsenal to slash my Spirit Core across his chest.

"You goddamn brat!" he screamed in vulgar outrage, jumping backward.

The wound on his chest was shallow. His skin was as hard as steel. *But I was able to cut him.* He had always seemed invincible, but I'd finally succeeded in injuring him, if only slightly. *All right! Heck yeah!*

A sense of euphoria filled me as it became clear that I'd grown as a swordsman.

"…I'll kill you," my Spirit Core seethed, veins bulging in his forehead. He enveloped himself in a cloak of darkness, just as I had.

"Ha-ha-ha… Amazing…," I muttered. His darkness was on another planet in both quality and quantity next to mine. It squirmed as if alive, making him look like some kind of terrifying bogeyman. The gap in our skill levels was so great that all I could do was laugh.

He followed that by producing the genuine black sword.

"…"

Chairwoman Reia had told me about it, but this was my first time seeing the real thing. *I want it.* The mock black sword I had worked so hard to obtain felt like an ordinary stick by comparison. It paled next to that ebon blade of his. *I want that weapon and power for myself!* I thought, staring at it with envy.

"Quit daydreamin', punk."

Just then, he was right in front of me, his sword raised overhead.

"Huh?!"

On reflex, I brought my sword horizontal in a defensive stance.

"Take this!"

Despite my efforts, the true black sword cut through my mock black sword as if it were made of cheese.

"Gah!" I shouted as he sliced open a gaping wound in my chest. My broken blade clattered to my feet.

"Ha, I was barely even tryin'. You're still weak as shit… You sure you're eatin' right?"

I heard him taunt me as I collapsed to the ground. Blood slowly spread slowly around me, and ferocious pain tormented my body.

"Ha, ha-ha…," I chuckled, as a feeling of pure joy welled up from my heart.

"What the hell're you laughin' about? You've been defeated. Have you finally lost it?" he asked.

"No, it's just…when I think about how I've gotten strong enough for you to produce the black sword…it makes me happy…," I responded.

About four months had passed since I began Soul Attire training. Just four short months. That time had passed in a flash, but I hadn't only succeeded in facing my Spirit Core—I had also managed to slightly cut his skin. Considering the snail's pace of my training in the billion-plus years I spent in the World of Time, this was shockingly fast growth.

The distance between him and me was shrinking clearly with each passing day. I could hardly contain the joy I felt about my progress.

"*Tch*… Don't get the wrong idea. I only showed you the real thing because you've been waving around that fake as if it's something to be proud of!" he shouted before he plunged the black sword down for a finishing blow, piercing my abdomen.

"Blargh!" Unfortunately, this session appeared to be over. "Ha-ha… I'll be back…," I murmured weakly.

He surprised me by speaking before I lost consciousness. Normally he only responded to me.

"I'll give you one warning. I won't be able to come to the surface for a while. I stayed out there too long last time and used a lot of spirit power. That body is important to me, so take care of it."

My mind then faded to black, and when I woke up, I had returned to the real world.

◼

Lunch break arrived after we'd finished our first and second period Soul Attire classes. I headed to the cafeteria as part of a large group of six people that consisted of me, Lia, Rose, Idora, Shido, and Cain. Lia's eyes lit up as soon as we stepped inside.

"Are you serious?! All the food here is *free*?!" she exclaimed.

"Yeah. White Lily students and staff get to use the cafeteria without being charged," Idora replied with a nod.

"Woo-hoo! Can I please have three Deluxe Special Bentos?" Lia asked, sounding incredibly excited. Morning classes had evidently made her hungry.

The man behind the counter stared at her openmouthed, unable to believe a slender girl like her had asked for so much food. "Th-three of them? Are you sure? The servings are pretty generous," he informed her.

"Yes, I'm sure!"

"C-coming right up..."

Lia's order kicked off an unfortunate chain of events.

"Three Deluxe Special Bentos, huh? Gimme four," Shido requested, suddenly getting competitive.

"Whuh! Excuse me, can I please change my order to five?" Lia ordered.

"Sorry, I meant six," Shido said.

"Oh, my apologies. I actually wanted seven," Lia declared.

They were both competitive as they came, and neither showed any signs of backing down.

"Tch... Gimme eight!" Shido yelled.

"Grr... nine, please!" Lia shouted.

""Ten bentos!"" they demanded simultaneously.

"You lookin' for a fight, blondie?!" Shido snapped.

"You're the one who started this!" Lia fired back.

And finally, they started arguing. *Come on, cut that out...* Fighting here would cause trouble for the people lined up behind us. Feeling like I had no choice, I attempted to play peacemaker.

"Hey, guys, calm down... Ten bentos is a ridiculous amount of food," I said.

"What are you talking about? That's a perfectly manageable amount," Lia responded, looking puzzled.

"...I guess it is." Changing her mind on that point was going to be impossible. Lia actually wasn't pushing herself at all; she probably *could* scarf down ten bentos in no time. That meant Shido was the one I needed to convince to back down. "Shido, I think you're a little out of your league here…," I said, trying to gently tell him that he had no chance.

"You cheeky little… You tryin' to say she can defeat the great Shido?" he responded angrily. All I'd done was pour oil on the fire.

I'm ninety-nine percent sure Shido has no chance of winning, but… This would only get more out of hand if I said that. We had caused enough trouble for the students behind us already.

"Haah… Have it your way," I said with a quiet sigh, giving up on trying to persuade them.

They both ended up ordering ten Deluxe Special Bentos. I got a nori bento, Rose got a seasonal autumn bento, Idora got a special beef bento, and Cain ordered a nori bento like me. Bentos were far from the only option on the menu, but after seeing Lia and Shido make such a big fuss over them, the rest of us couldn't help but get one ourselves.

""""""Let's dig in!""""""

We all put our hands together and started our lunches.

"Man, this hits the spot!" I exclaimed after savoring a bite of thick, deep-fried fish. Nori bentos were my favorite kind. The best thing about them was their usually cheap price. The "Discount Nori Bento" sold at Grand Swordcraft Academy had served me well back in my middle school days. The one served here contained dried bonito flakes and rice under roasted seaweed, along with seaweed-wrapped fried *chikuwa*.

"I am sitting at the same table as God, eating the same food as God… I can't believe this is happening. I might die from happiness…" Cain hugged himself with both arms and writhed with joy. He had always been a little weird.

"Hmm, this is pretty good," Rose commented with a satisfied nod after eating a bamboo shoot.

"The food here is delicious," Idora remarked, eating her bento with refined manners.

Meanwhile, as we enjoyed our lunches peacefully…

"Mmm, this is heavenly!"

"Haah, haah... You can really pack it in..."

...Lia and Shido were having an intense eating contest. Well, it was intense on Shido's part—Lia seemed totally unaware that any kind of competition was occurring. Instead, she was simply satisfying her massive appetite by chowing down on the food in front of her. Shido, on the other hand, was frantically scarfing down his portions in an attempt to keep up, but it looked like he was already struggling.

It wasn't long before the contest came to an end.

"Whoo, what a feast!" Lia said after easily polishing off all ten bentos.

"...Grk." Next to her, a dead-eyed Shido carried rice to his mouth with a trembling hand. He still had two Deluxe Special Bentos to go. He was finished.

"...Ha. You're... pretty good...," he managed before passing out.

"Sh-Shido? Are you okay?" I asked. I timidly shook his shoulders, but he didn't respond. He had completely blacked out. "*Haah*... I tried to warn you..." I sighed at the totally predictable outcome.

"...Do you mind if I say a few words to defend Shido's honor, my God?" Cain asked me with an uncharacteristically serious expression.

"N-no. What is it?"

"If you think only in terms of the eating contest, then yes, Shido was utterly humiliated. But please, take a close look at him. He's still gripping his chopsticks even after losing consciousness! That means his mind has not yet accepted defeat!"

"W-wow, so he is!" Shido's unyielding fighting spirit was truly impressive. "I could learn from his mental toughness..."

"You continue to impress me, my God! Your desire to improve is even more insatiable than I thought!" Cain exclaimed.

As Cain and I chatted, I happened to overhear a conversation between Idora and Rose.

"Allen's a little stupid, isn't he?" Idora asked.

"Hmm, I wouldn't say stupid. He's just…a bit of an airhead sometimes," Rose answered.

That was kind of rude.

Leaving an unconscious Shido alone, the rest of us spent lunch engaging in lighthearted conversation. Eventually, Idora said something that caught my attention.

"Oh yeah, the Skills Challenge is tomorrow. It'll be fun with you all participating," she said.

The Skills Challenge? Now that I thought about it, Chairwoman Reia might have mentioned something like that. "Sorry, but what's the Skills Challenge?" I asked, my interest piqued.

"It's a competition where White Lily students are measured across ten categories, including sword speed, arm strength, leg strength, short-range attack power, long-range attack power, and more. It's held once a month, and the top performer in each class year receives a certificate," Idora explained.

"…Competition?" Shido abruptly sprang to life. "Ha, that sounds fun! I'm gonna crush the shit out of you all!"

What the heck was he talking about? *All we're doing is measuring our skills… How is he going to 'crush the shit' out of anyone?* Anything and everything was a competition to this guy.

"Hey, that sounds fun! You all are going down!" Lia asserted.

"I can't possibly back down from a challenge," imparted Rose.

"You're on," Idora responded.

Lia and the headstrong girls accepted Shido's challenge immediately. I glanced at Cain.

"I will do as my God commands," he said, speaking his usual nonsense.

All I want to do is measure my abilities in peace…, I thought, and noticed everyone was staring at me.

"Are you game, Allen?" Lia asked.

"This is a chance to redeem myself, Allen!" Rose exclaimed.

"It'll be lame if you don't join us!" Shido pressed.

"I'll get you back for beating me last time!" Idora proclaimed.

It seemed like I had no escape. "Haah... Fine. I'll join your competition," I said with resignation.

That was how Lia, Rose, Shido, Idora, Cain, and I decided to battle it out for the highest score in the following day's Skills Challenge.

■

Morning arrived. All of the White Lily Girls Academy first-years had gathered in the immense schoolyard for the Skills Challenge.

"E-everyone looks so much more serious about this than I expected...," Lia remarked, seeming intimidated.

"...That's for sure," I responded.

The White Lily students looked like soldiers standing at attention, each one in quiet concentration. The tension was so thick, you could cut it with a knife. As soon as the first period bell rang, a student stepped up onto a small platform.

"It is time to begin the sixth Skills Challenge of the year," she announced. The student had a band around her right arm that read P.E. COMMITTEE. The Physical Education Committee must have been in charge of running the Skills Challenge. "We have some first-time participants this month, so I'll start with a basic explanation of the proceedings. Please remain quiet until I am finished."

She then gave a basic rundown of the rules. There were ten categories in the Skills Challenge, and each one was scored on a scale of one to one hundred. Students competed to achieve the highest total score. The use of Soul Attire was allowed in every category. The student with the highest score in each year received a shield and a certificate. This all matched what Idora had told us yesterday. A broadcast echoed throughout the schoolyard once the P.E. committee member had finished her address.

"*Ah, ah, mic check, mic check. All right, we're good! The Broadcasting*

Club you all know and love will be providing commentary for today's competition!" The announcer had a slight northern accent—like Ferris and Rize did—and I got the impression that she really enjoyed hearing herself talk. *"Are you all as excited as I am? But before we kick off today's hotly anticipated Skills Challenge, I have some mega-famous guests to introduce!"*

The White Lily students all turned our way upon hearing those words.

"First up is the juvenile delinquent from Ice King Academy—Shido Jukuriuuuus! He's such a bad boy that he was suspended twice in his first semester of high school! But that doesn't change the fact that he's one of the strongest first-years in the country!"

The students in Shido's vicinity backed away from him after his introduction.

"Oh my god, do you see that wicked look in his eyes?!"

"Oh, so he's the thug everyone's been talking about."

"H-he's terrifying…"

I couldn't really blame them; I found Shido difficult to approach even as a fellow guy. The girls' reactions were unsurprising.

"This next person needs no introduction! He's the infamous villain of Thousand Blade Academy—Allen Rodooool! He defeated Big Sis Idora, which makes him our sworn enemy!"

Everyone stared at me after that slightly malicious introduction.

"…Huh? Doesn't he look a bit nicer than the last guy?"

"Look at that black and white hair, though. No decent person has a dye job like that."

"Don't forget he defeated Big Sis! We can't underestimate him!"

I clearly wasn't particularly welcome here.

"Now for everyone's favorite part—it's betting time! Write your name, class, number, and the amount you want to wager on the ticket you were given last week, then put it in one of the boxes in front of the platform!" the broadcaster instructed.

I looked toward the platform and saw three big boxes with names written on them. The yellow box said IDORA LUKSMARIA, the blue box said SHIDO JUKURIUS, and the black box said ALLEN RODOL.

"There's no way Big Sis will lose!"

"I'm voting for her, too, of course!"

The White Lily students all pulled white slips of paper out of their pockets and put them in Idora's box. Her box quickly filled to capacity, while my and Shido's boxes remained totally empty.

"They're...betting?" I muttered, and Idora explained the situation.

"Yep. It's a Skills Challenge tradition for students to wager on who they think will finish first in their year. Oh yeah, you guys haven't gotten tickets yet. Just ask the P.E. Committee representative for one."

"O-okay..."

The White Lily students seemed very confident that Idora would win. They would be rooting heavily against me and Shido.

"Hrm... I'm gonna place a bet!" Lia announced.

"Allen is objectively the only choice," Rose said with a chuckle.

They both got tickets from the P.E. committee member, wrote *100,000 guld* and *Allen Rodol*, and placed them in the black box.

"O-one hundred thousand guld?!" I shouted, stunned by how much they bet. "A-are you sure you want to do that?!"

""What do you mean?"" they responded simultaneously in confusion. They seemed to have no idea how much money that was.

"Hold on... H-how can you possibly be so calm about this?! You both bet one hundred thousand guld!" I exclaimed.

One hundred thousand guld was a *lot* of money. You could easily live off of that amount for a month. It would last three to four months in Goza Village. Considering how frugally I lived, I bet I could stretch it out for at least a year.

"You're overreacting, Allen. One hundred thousand guld isn't much," Lia said.

"Yeah, it's nothing to get worked up about," Rose agreed.

"Huh...," I responded.

I always forgot about how filthy rich the two of them were because I spent so much time with them. Lia was a Vesterian princess, and I heard that Rose had made a ton of money in her days as a bounty hunter. My family was very poor, so their sense of what was expensive or not wildly diverged from mine.

"Besides, there's no way you're going to lose," Lia added.

"There's no question about that," Rose said.

They both nodded confidently.

"...Well, I'll do my best." Their trust in me made me genuinely happy.

The odds were revealed after a short wait. I was 50-1, Shido was 55-1, and Idora was 1.1-1.

I can't believe my eyes. It was true that gambling wasn't illegal in Liengard, but it was unreal seeing an entire school year participate in such large-scale betting, and in broad daylight at that. *It may not be illegal, but is it not against school rules?* I thought with unease.

"Hey, what is going on here?!" Chairwoman Kemmi ran to the schoolyard in a mad dash. "What are you all so excited about? Explain yourself!" she yelled, grabbing a member of the P.E. Committee. The girl told her what was going on. "...Oh, I see. I'll take one of those."

Kemmi snatched a ticket from the girl, wrote *1,000,000 guld,* and shoved it into the box with ALLEN RODOL written on it. The chairwoman herself had joined in on the gambling, and she'd even put her money on a student from a rival school. Neither one of those things was a good look for the head of White Lily.

"Ch-Chairwoman?! Why did you bet on Allen Rodol instead of Big Sis?!"

"You're the worst! Traitor!"

Unsurprisingly, the White Lily students proceeded to browbeat her.

"*Haah...* You girls don't understand a thing. I might as well take this moment to teach you all a valuable lesson. Typically, you bet on the person with the *best* odds of winning when you're gambling," she said without a hint of guilt.

"Are you saying Allen Rodol is better than Big Sis?!"

"You shameless… You're betraying Big Sis—no, all of White Lily Girls Academy!"

The criticism from the White Lily students grew even more intense.

"Hmph! I don't care what you all have to say! Allen is the clear favorite! You saw the Sword Master Festival, right? Idora doesn't stand a chance!" Kemmi doubled down.

…Yeah, she was the kind of person who was better off keeping her mouth shut. All she did was pour oil on an already raging fire, and the jeering grew even louder.

The announcer cut through the noise with a somewhat forceful tone. *"A-attention, please! Now that we've all gotten fired up, let's go ahead and start the Skills Challenge! The first category is short-range attack power!"* she announced.

A group of students carried an ungainly four-sided machine to the schoolyard from a shed next to the gym as the MC spoke. There was a target on the front side and an LCD panel installed above it.

"All you have to do in this category is approach the machine and unleash your strongest short-range attack. The results of the measurement will be shown on the LCD panel up top. The stronger the attack, the higher the number! Okay, anyone who's ready can step right up!" the announcer said, finishing her explanation.

"You really think that cheap piece of junk can measure my unrivaled strength?" Shido boasted, walking up to the machine full of confidence.

"Stay focused, Shido!" Cain encouraged.

"I'll destroy this thing with one blow. Consume—Ice Wolf Vanargand!" Frigid air filled the schoolyard the moment he summoned his Soul Attire. "Vanar Slash!" He performed an explosively fast thrust on the machine, cold air gushing from his pommel. "What the hell?!" To Shido's surprise, however, the measuring device didn't budge.

"Oh my goodness! That's ninety-four points. We already have a score in the nineties! Ice King's Shido Jukurius truly is prolific!"

The White Lily students all gasped after the broadcaster read the score on the LCD screen. Judging by that reaction, ninety-four was a really good score.

"I'm going next," Idora said competitively, walking briskly up to the measuring device. She had already summoned her Soul Attire, Neba Grome.

"Flying Thunder—Maximum One Hundred Million Volts!" Blue lightning surrounded her body as she slowly lifted her sword overhead. "Thunderclap Style—Purple Lightning!" She struck the machine with a downward diagonal slash as fast as lightning.

"Her score is—ninety-three points! That's unfortunately one less than Shido Jukurius's score!" the broadcaster said.

Idora had been close, but she failed to reach Shido's score.

"N-no way…" She drooped her shoulders.

"Ha, you don't stand a chance against me," Shido boasted with a smile.

Now that Shido and Idora had gone, I was up next. I could feel everyone's eyes on me.

…All right. Let's do this. I stood before the measuring device, drew my sword, and paused when a harrowing possibility occurred to me. *Accidents do happen… I should ask, just in case.* I sheathed my sword and turned toward Kemmi.

"Excuse me, can I ask a question?" I asked.

"Yes, you may. What is it?" Kemmi responded.

"If I break this machine… Will I have to pay for it?"

I needed to make sure I wouldn't be held accountable for it. I wasn't filthy rich like everyone else here, so I had to be more careful than most when it came to money.

"Ah-ha-ha, you're such a worrywart, Allen. You have nothing to fear.

The Anti-Impact Machine mk3 is completely indestructible," the chair-woman declared.

"Let's say I get unlucky and break it anyway... Can you assure me I won't have to pay for it?" I asked again.

"Yes. I would never expect that of a student. Forget about that, though. Use that wicked darkness you displayed at the Sword Master Festival to beat Shido's ninety-four! ...I have one million guld riding on you—literally my entire fortune—so please give this your all."

Kemmi pushed me toward the measuring device. The last thing she'd said to me threw me off for a second, but I decided not to worry about it. Now that I knew I wouldn't have to pay for any damages, I drew my blade and coated it in darkness to create the mock black sword.

...This feels good. My control of the darkness has improved a little. It used to take all my effort to cloak my body in it, but now I could direct it onto a specific target like my limbs or my sword. This would allow me to lower the rate at which I consumed the darkness, letting me fight with it for longer.

"Good luck, Allen!"

"Show them the strength of Thousand Blade!"

Lia and Rose cheered me on. I waved in response and faced the measuring device once again.

...Shido got a ninety-four, and Idora got a ninety-three. I would need to get a ninety-five or more to beat them. *Phew... let's do this.*

Duels between swordsmen were nothing to scoff at. No matter the type of competition, you needed to give your all to win. I tightened my grip on my mock black blade, assumed the middle stance, steadied my breath—and took a huge step forward.

"Fifth Style—World Render!"

I performed my most powerful attack—so strong, it could cut through space—and sliced the measuring device in two. The severed top half of the measuring device read *100*.

"I knew that was gonna happen..."

It turned out that the ostensibly indestructible machine couldn't withstand an attack that could cut through the fabric of space. I couldn't help but chuckle at the predictable outcome. A wave of relief washed over me as well.

Thank goodness...

Measuring devices could be shockingly expensive. I was glad Kemmi had promised me that I wouldn't have to pay for it.

"I-I can't believe my eyes! Allan just cut the Anti-Impact Machine mk3 clean in two! What a tragic end for the so-called indestructible machine! That strike produced an astounding score of one hundred! Allen Rodol is the real deal. It's no accident he beat Big Sis!" the announcer gushed excitedly. The surrounding first-years sent angry stares my way.

Ah-ha-ha... Should've known they'd be upset about me beating Idora..., I thought, feeling a little uncomfortable.

"Damn you, Allen...," Shido seethed.

"You're...really good...!" Idora admitted.

They both glared at me. They were really competitive.

"I-I got lucky... That could've gone either way!" I said quickly. I wouldn't have put it past either one of them to challenge me to a duel on the spot if I'd angered them any more. I gave them an inoffensive response to avoid that fate.

"Y-you can't be serious... How could this happen to my Anti-Impact Machine mk3?!" Kemmi muttered, looking crestfallen.

"...Huh? What do you mean by 'my'?" I asked.

"The chairwoman made that measuring device herself. It might be hard to believe, but she's a genius scientist," Idora explained. Now *that* was a bombshell.

"She's a scientist?! That's amazing...," I responded. I couldn't believe this gambling addict was that talented... It just went to show you should never judge a book by its cover.

The short-range attack power measurements continued after the Anti-Impact Machine mk2 was rolled out of the shed. The earlier model differed only in its durability and appearance—the measuring program within the machine was exactly the same, so the swap would have no impact on the scoring.

The broadcaster spoke up once all the first-years had obtained their short-range attack measurements. *"It's time for the second category, long-range attack power! You all will face the measuring device from a distance of thirty meters and perform a long-range attack! The stronger the move, the higher the score the LCD screen will display. Hit it with everything you've got!"*

The P.E. Committee members stepped forward to draw a white line thirty meters from the measuring device.

"I kinda suck at long-range attacks, but I'll give it a go..."

Shido scratched his head and stood on the white line. He was up first again.

"Eat this—Freezing Spear!"

He swung Vanargand downward to create a spear of ice, then hurled it toward the measuring device. It struck the middle of the machine.

"And the score is—eighty-three! It's more difficult to earn points in the long-range attack category than in the short-range attack category, so Shido's score is nothing to sneeze at!"

The score looked underwhelming compared to the ninety-four he'd got in the previous category, but this was a long-range attack. As the announcer said, eighty-three probably wasn't bad.

"*Tch*, goddammit..." Shido clicked his tongue loudly, clearly upset with his score.

"I'm going next," Idora said. She stood quietly on the line, looking determined to make up for her narrow defeat in the previous category. Then she used Flying Thunder to envelop herself in a high-pressure electrical current and lifted a lance overhead. The next moment, a giant bolt of lightning descended from the cloudless sky and struck the tip of her lance.

Th-this move... This was the strongest technique she'd performed at the Sword Master Festival.

"One Hundred Million Volts—Imperata Grome!"

Idora struck the center of the measuring device with a spiraling azure lightning attack. The electricity kicked up a cloud of sand and filled the courtyard with a burning smell.

"And the score is—Ninety-five?! That's a stunningly high number! That's Big Sis for you! She's the pride of White Lily Girls Academy!" the MC said, and the first-years cheered.

Incredible... She beat Shido by twelve whole points... Her score was astonishing.

"Hah, I win," Idora said to Shido, wearing a boastful grin. She even taunted him by making a peace sign with her fingers. She was getting him back for beating her the last time.

"Bullshit! I beat you in the short-range category! I'm gonna pulverize you!" Shido screamed.

"If you add the short-range and long-range results, I have 188 and you have 177. I beat you handily."

"We've only done two categories, though!"

"Yeah, yeah. Good luck catching up."

"Damn you..."

...These two might be more alike than I thought. I stepped onto the white line thirty meters from the measuring device and unleashed my power. Wicked darkness gushed forth from my body, painting the entirety of White Lily Girls Academy black.

"Wh-what the heck?!"

"That's the darkness Allen used during the Sword Master Festival... There's no way it was this strong before, though!"

"What a repulsive power..."

The White Lily students looked on in shock as the blackness raced across the ground. Their comments strengthened a conviction of mine.

...I knew it. The darkness has *gotten stronger.*

I thought back to something Dodriel had said—that Soul Attire was strengthened when you toed the line separating life from death. A few days ago, I'd miraculously survived being stabbed through the heart. That experience might have brought my body and soul closer together, giving me easier access to *his* darkness.

…This feels good. The gloom was adapting to my body. It felt right, like I had been living with this power my entire life. *I think I'm gonna get a good score!* I enveloped my body in a cloak of black, lifted the mock ebon blade overhead, and—

"S-stop!"

—Kemmi shouted at me to hold off.

"Um, is something wrong?" I asked.

"There's no way my precious Anti-Impact Machine mk2 will survive an attack that powerful! I'll just give you a one hundred, so please put away that dreadful sword!" she yelled, pale-faced.

"D-do I have to…?" I looked at the surrounding students.

"You're overstepping, Chairwoman!"

"Are you suggesting he can beat Big Sis's incredible score of ninety-five?! You're a traitor!"

"I see right through you, Chairwoman! You're trying to give Allen the win so you can get rich! You bet a million guld on him!"

The crowd of first-years bashed Kemmi with angry protests.

"Um…I'm gonna go ahead, okay?" I said.

"…Fine," Kemmi responded dejectedly.

I feel kinda bad for her… She clearly had her work cut out for her if she wanted to gain the trust of her students. *Oops, I need to focus on the task at hand.* I cleared my mind, took a deep breath, and swung my blade with determination.

"Sixth Style—Dark Boom!"

I produced an enormous black slash attack and felt an unprecedented amount of recoil in my arms. *Wow, that's huge!* The dark slash attack was over twice as large as usual. It tore apart the earth as it raced forward and reduced the Anti-Impact Machine mk2 to rubble.

"N-nooo…," Kemmi cried in despair as the measuring device clanged to the ground in metal fragments. A *100* was barely visible on the cracked LCD screen.

"I-is this guy human?! What overwhelming strength! I've never seen a perfect score on the long-range attack!" the announcer proclaimed, her voice echoing across the quiet courtyard. I looked around to see many of the female students frozen with their mouths agape.

"You've gotten much stronger since the Sword Master Festival…," Shido said.

"What kind of training regimen are you on, Allen?!" Idora exclaimed.

They both gritted their teeth in frustration.

"You never cease to amaze, Allen! That was an incredible attack!" Lia praised.

"You emerged from that life-or-death struggle even stronger than before… You really are something else," Rose added.

Lia and Rose looked proud.

Afterward, the dusty Anti-Impact Machine mk1 was rolled out of the shed, and the long-range attack measurements recommenced. We spent the next few hours testing a variety of categories including sword speed, leg strength, and reaction time, and once that was through, it was time for the results to be announced. I glanced at the clock tower and saw it was already past five in the afternoon. It wasn't long until sunset.

"All right, it's time to announce the total score for each of the betting targets: Idora Luksmaria, Shido Jukurius, and Allen Rodol!" the broadcaster said loudly. The schoolyard grew tense.

I had lost track of my total score in the process of performing the ten categories. I was nervous as well as I waited to hear the results.

"First, Idora Luksmaria of White Lily Girls Academy scored…950 points! A score of 900 is astounding, and she surpassed it by 50 points! Absolutely incredible!"

The female students all celebrated the result.

"That's our Big Sis! Only legends can score in the 900s!"

"She'll beat that damn Allen Rodol for sure!"

You could score up to 1,000 points in the Skills Challenge, so Idora's score was tremendously high.

"Next up, Shido Jukurius of Ice King Academy scored...947 points! She did it! Big Sis beat Shido!"

"Tch."

Shido clicked his tongue in frustration after learning of his defeat.

Only three points. They were really close... Shido had beaten Idora in most of the categories after the long-range attack. He definitely would have beaten her if the winner had been determined by the number of categories won, but his twelve-point deficit from the long-range attack measurement had proved too difficult to overcome.

"Last but not least, Allen Rodol of Thousand Blade Academy scored...975 points?! This is a ridiculously high score! This might be an all-time record for White Lily Girls Academy!"

A chilling silence befell the courtyard.

"...Shit...," Shido cursed, kicking the rubble of the Anti-Impact Machine mk2.

"I lost again...," Idora muttered, slumping her shoulders in disappointment.

"I bet one million guld on Allen on 50:1 odds... That means I get fifty million guld! Ha-ha-ha... Mwa-ha-ha-ha-ha!" Meanwhile, Kemmi cackled like a sleazy villain after realizing the amount of money she had raked in. "I'm gonna buy beer and snacks and hit the casino... It's time for a weekend spending spree! Yahoo!"

She sprinted excitedly around the school yard like a small child. I got the sense she was going to be broke by next week.

"Allen Rodol will receive a shield and a certificate at a later date for achieving the top score among the first-years. That marks the end of this year's sixth Skills Challenge. Have a good night!"

With the competition over, my friends and I headed to the cafeteria for a slightly early dinner, then used White Lily's spacious schoolyard to train. Lia and Rose reviewed their Hegemonic School of Swordcraft and Cherry Blossom Blade School of Swordcraft forms, respectively. Shido intently practiced long-range attacks, Cain happily performed practice swings next to me, and Idora manipulated lightning with tight precision.

...*Man, this is fun.* There was nothing I loved more than working on my swordcraft alongside other people. How happy I would be if time froze so I could bask in this moment forever.

We decided to split up a few hours later at sunset.

"See you tomorrow, Lia, Rose, and Idora," I said.

"Good night, Allen," Lia responded.

"See you," Rose said.

"Night," Idora added.

The male and female dorms were in opposite directions, so we parted ways with the girls in the schoolyard.

"Good night, Shido and Cain," I said.

"Mmhmm," Shido grunted.

"I'll never forget the incredible time I was able to spend with you today, my God," Cain responded.

I parted ways with the two of them inside the dorm for male faculty members, then entered the room I'd been assigned.

"I'm home," I announced to the empty room. Naturally, no one responded. *I feel kinda lonely without Lia.* Staying with her wasn't an option outside of Thousand Blade, though. "Man, I'm beat..."

I was exhausted from the strenuous Skills Challenge and the hours of practice swings I performed afterward. *Guess I'll take a bath and go to bed a little early...* I stretched, and someone knocked on my door.

Who would come to my room this late...? Is it Lia? I thought as I opened the door.

"Hey, Allen."

It was none other than Idora, wearing a small backpack.

"Idora...? What are you doing here so late?" I asked.

"Can I come in?" she responded.

"U-uh, sure."

"Thanks."

Getting an ominous premonition, I invited the unexpected guest into my room.

■

I poured some cold tea from the fridge for us.

"Here you go," I said.

"Thanks," she responded.

Idora sat at the table and gracefully sipped her beverage. Then...

"..."

"..."

...We sat there in awkward silence.

What should I do...? Was it on me as the guy to bring up something interesting? *No, wait. Idora is the one who came all the way here.* She must have had something she wanted to talk about. *This silence is super awkward... But I shouldn't rush her. Waiting for her to speak is definitely the right call!*

After reaching that decision, I sat there and waited for her to say something. Idora didn't look especially uncomfortable, herself. She was wearing her usual blank expression, which made it difficult to tell what she was thinking.

"..."

"..."

Three agonizing minutes passed.

"Um...Idora? What brings you to my room so late? Can I do something for you?" I asked timidly, finally breaking the silence. Facing a girl wordlessly for that length of time was more than I could handle.

"Oh, yeah. I have something I want to talk about... But can I ask you a question first?" Idora requested.

"Yes, you may," I responded.

"I've noticed you act stiffly around me. Why is that?"

"...Huh?"

I was taken aback by her unexpected question.

"We're the same age. There's no reason to treat me any differently than anyone else."

"I...guess so."

There wasn't any particular reason why I tried to be polite with her. *Hmm, I'm not sure how to answer that.* I felt like I would've sounded unfriendly if I told her my attitude simply reflected that we hadn't known each other for very long, and saying "I'm not sure" wasn't going to cut it as an explanation, either.

"Um... I just think it's best to treat girls with respect...," I said, ultimately deciding to go with a safe answer.

"But you don't act that way around Lia and Rose. I'd prefer if you to treat me like a friend, too, if you don't mind," Idora requested, looking somewhat pitiful as she said that.

There was no reason to deny her request. If she wanted me to act casually around her, that was fine with me.

"Got it. W-we're friends, Idora," I stammered shyly. Having this kind of conversation with a girl was a little embarrassing. She smiled happily, not seeming to care.

"Yeah. Friends," Idora repeated. She then stood up and walked toward the door. "See you tomorrow."

"Huh...? Oh, uh, good night," I responded. That was a bit of a letdown; I hadn't thought that would be the whole reason for her visit.

Idora put on her shoes and grabbed the doorknob before she paused and said, "Oh, I forgot." Then she took her shoes back off and returned to the table. "That's not what I came here to talk about."

"O-okay," I responded.

She really is an airhead..., I thought. Idora softly cleared her throat.

"*Ahem*. Now, on to the reason for my visit."

"Go ahead."

"Let's see... I've been training hard since losing to you in the Sword Master Festival. But during the Skills Challenge today, I could tell that the gap between us has grown." She looked at me, frustration clear on her face. "I'm thinking you must have a secret."

"A secret?"

"Yeah. There must be some secret behind your strength. I want you to answer my questions honestly." Idora took a piece of paper out of her small backpack. It had a list of questions written on it in neat handwriting. She'd come prepared. "...Do you mind?" she asked.

"No, not at all," I answered. I was happy to cooperate if responding to her questions would help her.

"Thanks. First question—your swordcraft is very unique. Who was your teacher?"

"..."

A tough question right off the bat.

"Ah-ha-ha... It's embarrassing, but I'm self-taught."

Typically, swordfighters would join schools of swordcraft to learn the fundamentals of their weapon. That was expected of everyone who took up the blade. People like me, who hadn't been accepted into a school of swordcraft, however, had no choice but to teach themselves. Society ridiculed such exceptions, deeming them "Reject Swordsmen."

"Self-taught? Why? Could you not find a good teacher?" Idora asked, tilting her head in confusion. She was unaware of my humble beginnings.

"...Not a single instructor accepted me. They all insisted I had no talent," I explained to her.

"But you're so strong now... Those instructors were all clueless." Idora moved on to the next question with disbelief on her face.

How long do you spend on swordcraft every day?
How many swordcraft manuals have you read?
How many meals do you eat a day?

I answered each one politely, my startlement growing as the list of inquiries climbed over ten.

"This is my last question. What kind of training have you spent the most time on since the Sword Master Festival?"

"The type of training I spent the most time on..."

"Yeah."

Idora nodded with great interest. This must have been the question she was most curious about if she'd saved it for last.

Hmm... My daily training regime covered many different areas, including fighting my Spirit Core, working on my control of the darkness, and weightlifting, but...

"Probably practice swings."

...I was sure that was what I spent the most time on. I never slacked on getting my swings in, without exception.

"...Give me a serious answer," Idora said, glaring at me. She was clearly unsatisfied with my response.

"I was being serious...," I insisted. I was telling the truth. There was no doubt that I dedicated most of my daily training time to practice swings.

"...I see. You're set on hiding the secret of your strength," she muttered, looking sullen.

"I'm not trying to do that, honest..."

The first thing that had crossed my mind when Idora mentioned the "secret of my strength" was the 100-Million-Year Button. Chairwoman Reia had forbidden me from telling anyone about it, though, so I couldn't bring it up. *I feel bad, but there's nothing I can do about that.* The chairwoman had told me that the Black Organization was after the 100-Million-Year Button. I could put Idora in danger if I wasn't careful. Guilty conscience or no, I couldn't tell her about the button.

"...Fine. I'll just observe your daily routine," Idora said. I wasn't sure what she meant by that.

"O-observe...?" I repeated.

"Yeah. I'm going to watch you to learn exactly how you became so powerful."

"Oh, that's what you mean."

I was a little thrown off by the word "observe," but watching and learning from others was a fundamental part of swordcraft. You didn't need to ask someone's permission to do that. I had mimicked Rose's Cherry Blossom Blade School of Swordcraft, myself.

"...Do you mind?"

"No, not at all. I can't guarantee you'll learn anything useful, though."

"Good... Okay, that's everything I had to say. Thanks for your help." Idora smiled happily, then made a shocking power play. "I'm gonna take a bath."

"Sure, go ahead... Wait, wait?!" I exclaimed.

She had changed the topic so quickly that someone else might have missed it. Idora had deftly tricked me into giving her permission to use my bath.

"H-hold on! What do you mean by that?!" I shouted.

"Huh? Do you not know what a bath is...?" Idora responded.

"Sorry... I phrased that poorly. I'm not asking you what a bath is, I'm asking why you're taking one in my dorm room," I explained.

"I told you. I'm going to observe your daily routine," she said flippantly.

"My daily routine... Do you actually intend to watch my every action?!"

"Yep."

Idora looked thrown off by my surprise. *Oh yeah, I totally forgot...* Her communication skills were hopeless.

"Does that mean you're spending the night here?"

"Of course. That's what this bag is for."

Idora proudly pulled a set of cute yellow pajamas from her bag. It seemed like she'd planned on staying in my room from the start.

"I-I don't think that's the best idea..."

A lot could go wrong with a teenage boy and girl sleeping under the same roof. Lia and I...were different. We were master and servant, so our situation was hardly normal.

"Are you...dating someone, Allen?" Idora asked, tilting her head uneasily.

"I'm not, but..." I trailed off. Lia and I didn't have that kind of relationship...yet.

"...Good." Idora breathed a sigh of relief for some reason and headed for the changing room. "I'm gonna get in the bath." She closed the curtain behind her.

"I-Idora, wait!"

I grabbed the curtain in a panic, and heard rustling from the other side. "Huh?!" She had already started taking off her clothes. *Crap, there's nothing I can do now...* Now that she was naked, the thin cloth curtain might as well have been made of steel. I was powerless to stop her.

"*Haah...* Why did this have to happen...?"

I let out a small sigh and heard her humming from the bathroom. A girl my age—and one of unrivaled beauty, at that—was showering in my dorm room. The thought set my heart racing... *This is stressing me out.*

After fifteen long minutes, I heard the bathroom door creak open. *Phew, she's done...*

I heaved a sigh of relief...

"Hey, Allen. Where are the towels?"

...Only to see Idora pull back the curtain without hesitation while she was still stark naked.

"Wh-whuh?!"

I saw her dripping wet hair, her flushed cheeks, her bewitching limbs, and most shockingly, her fully exposed lady bits. I immediately turned around and shut my eyes tight.

"Wh-wh-what are you doing?!" I yelled.

"Um... Asking you where the towels are?" she responded.

"I-I'll bring you one! Right now! Just get back in there and close the curtain!" I demanded.

"...? Okay," she muttered in confusion. Idora returned to the changing room and closed the curtain.

I made a mad dash to retrieve a towel from my dresser and offered it through a gap in the curtain.

"H-here you go..."

"Thanks."

Idora hummed and wiped herself dry without further conversation.

Haah... *Are all the students at girls-only schools like this?* She totally lacked any sense of caution around men. *Though to be fair, there can't be many people who can hurt the Wonder Child.* She'd let down her guard way too much, though. I was really worried that she was going to fall victim to a terrible crime one day.

After a few minutes, Idora emerged from the shower wearing cute yellow pajamas. Her moist skin, slightly flushed cheeks, and wet hair made her look a little more mature than usual... It was an alluring sight.

"Phew... I feel refreshed," she said.

"...Glad to hear it," I responded.

I resumed stretching, and Idora started to dry her hair.

"*Hraah...*" Idora yawned.

She quickly readied herself for sleep and then plopped onto my bed with another adorable yawn. Her eyes were so tired that it seemed like she would fall asleep at any moment.

"G'night, Allen...," she mumbled, wrapping herself in my blanket. Evidently, she was the type to get easily tuckered out at night.

"G-good night...," I responded.

After that, I took a relaxing bath and quickly got ready for bed. I turned toward Idora to find that she had balled up in the bed like a small child. She was breathing softly in her sleep.

"...Yep, she's leaving herself wide open."

I appreciated that she trusted me, but...she really needed to be more careful.

"I'll bring that up to her another time."

I decided to just get some shut-eye for now. I laid a bath towel on the floor to make a simple bed and lay down.

"Good night, Idora."

I turned off the lights with a remote control, closed my eyes, and dozed off.

■

I awoke to sunlight streaming in through an open window the next morning.

"Ngh..."

I gave a big stretch and slowly got up.

"Morning, Allen."

Idora smiled at me in her White Lily uniform.

"...G-good morning, Idora."

My breath caught in my throat at the novel sight of the beautiful Idora greeting me first thing in the morning, but I tried to act naturally so she wouldn't notice. I started toward the bathroom to brush my teeth.

"Can I make something?" Idora asked, pointing at the fridge.

"Sure, but...are you fine with cooking?" I asked guiltily.

"Yeah. Making food for two people is no harder than making food for one."

"Cool, thanks. You can take whatever you want from the fridge. There's not much in there, though."

I was pretty sure there wasn't much in the fridge besides eggs, bean sprouts, and pork.

"...This should do." Idora nodded after closely examining the contents of the fridge and set right to cooking.

I got ready for the day as she cooked. Idora called me right as I put my arms through my Thousand Blade uniform.

"It's ready, Allen."

"Thanks, I'm coming." I checked my appearance in the mirror and walked to the table where she was waiting. "Wow, this looks great!"

She'd made white rice with sunny-side-up eggs and a pork and bean sprout stir-fry. I was impressed that she had been able to whip up two dishes in such a short amount of time.

"Ha-ha, I hope you like it. Do you want soy sauce?"

"Yeah, thank you."

Idora and I sat at the table.

""Let's dig in.""

I pierced the swollen yolk with my chopsticks, causing yellow juice to spill outward. I then wrapped the soft-boiled yolk in the fried egg white and took a bite.

"How is it?" Idora asked.

"It's delicious! You're a great cook," I answered.

That was a bit surprising, given how unskilled many of the girls at Thousand Blade were at cooking.

"Glad you like it. I'm not much of a chef, though."

"Really? I think this is impressive, personally."

"I guess I'm good at small dishes like this. I can't handle sweet foods like cookies and cakes, though. I always end up adding a secret ingredient that turns them into horrible monstrosities. My cookies caused an incident in middle school."

"H-huh..." So Idora was the type of cook who excelled at making certain kinds of foods and was terrible at making others. "By the way, was your middle school also a girls-only school?"

"Yeah. My father is firmly opposed to mixed-gender education. He's always been a worrywart."

"Is he now…?" If her father saw us in this moment, I would be afraid for my life. "Anyway, Idora."

"What?"

"You can't tell anyone that you're staying in my room, okay?"

"Huh? I don't understand why, but okay."

I was a little worried that she didn't understand the importance of keeping this a secret… but I had no choice but to trust her.

After eating breakfast, we decided to go to school much earlier than usual to avoid anyone seeing us together. It was seven in the morning, which was two hours before first period.

No one will catch us at this time, I thought. How naive I was. I opened the door slowly and quietly…

"Oh, my God! How can I possibly express my joy at attending the same classes as you for the second day in a…row… Huh?!"

…And found Cain outside my door, kneeling and bowing his head. I had no idea how long he had been waiting there. He went speechless after seeing Idora emerge with me from my room.

"M-m-my God?! Wh-what is this?! Why was Idora in your room?!" Cain shrieked, eyeing each of us in turn.

"P-pipe down! She's only staying in my room temporarily for…for reasons! It's not what you think at all!"

"Understood."

He accepted my explanation shockingly little resistance.

"Uh, do you believe me…?" I asked.

"I am so foolish as to doubt the word of God. Whatever you say is the truth. That is all," Cain responded, accompanying his outrageous statement with a gentle smile. I had no idea why he worshipped me like this, but it was to my benefit this time.

"Anyway, please keep this between us," I requested.

"Of course, my God! I will keep your secret even if it costs me my life!" he promised, bowing to me in reverence.

With Cain successfully quieted, I headed for Class 1-A.

■

A week had passed since my transfer to White Lily Girls Academy.

"Good morning, Master Allen."

"Good morning, Allen."

"Morning, Shirley and Misha."

I was happy to now be on speaking terms with my classmates. They had been wary of me at first, but Idora helped me break the ice little by little, and now we were comfortable enough around one another to make small talk. I said good morning to the other girls, and the classroom door rattled open.

"Good morning, Allen!"

"…Mornin'."

An energetic Lia and a drowsy Rose walked through.

"Good morning," I responded.

"You've been getting to class much earlier than usual, Allen. Did something happen?" Lia asked after setting her things down at her desk. Her astute question threw me off

"N-no, nothing's happened! Everything's perfectly normal…"

"Hmm…?"

I darted my eyes away, and she stared at me closely.

No one has found out that I'm living with Idora…I think. Cain was the only one who knew, and he had kept his promise. *Just one more week… I just have to endure one more week…* All I could do was pray that nothing would happen.

A girl interrupted my thoughts by addressing me timidly.

"Um… Master Allen. May I ask you a question?"

I was pretty sure her name was Reese.

"Sure. What is it?" I responded.

"I have been wondering something about your darkness… Can it heal injuries?"

"Well spotted. This darkness can heal minor injuries in seconds flat." I nodded and summoned a bit of darkness at my fingertips.

"I knew it…!" She clapped her hands happily, and then her expression turned serious. "To be honest, I have a request for you. Would you be willing to give me a moment of your time?"

"A request…?"

"Yes. The thing is, I have a scar that has caused me a lot of distress. It's a bit unsightly, but please take a look…" She nervously rolled up one of her sleeves to reveal deep red teeth marks on her arm. "This is a wound I suffered five years ago when I was still in elementary school. I got it when we were hunting monsters during a class. I lost focus for the briefest of moments, and a werewolf bit me."

"That's terrible… I assume you've already seen a doctor about this?"

Liengard's medical technology was very advanced. A bite wound of this size could be healed in no time.

"Yes, of course. I have seen multiple doctors, but there was nothing any of them could do. This wound carries a monster's curse, which means modern medical technology cannot heal it. They said it would remain on my skin forever…," Reese muttered. She looked like she was going to burst into tears.

A curse, huh. That certainly makes things difficult… Some monsters had the mysterious power to inflict curses. Almost nothing was known about their effects, what triggered them, or how to dispel them.

"I had given up on healing it…but after witnessing that strange darkness of yours, I thought you might be able to do something. Could you please lend me that power, Master Allen?"

Reese bowed. I could hear the desperation in her voice.

"…Okay. I don't know how much I'll be able to do, but I'll give it a try," I responded.

This darkness was that *monster*'s power. I doubted it would work, but there was no harm in trying.

"Th-thank you very much…!"

"Are you ready?"

"Yes, go ahead."

I concentrated and covered her discolored right arm in darkness. I was filled with both a tender sensation and the nasty feeling of having swallowed something filthy. The darkness quickly returned Reese's dark red skin to its original, unblemished state.

""""A-amazing…""""

The girls watching around us gasped in admiration at the magical sight.

"Phew… Looks like it worked," I said.

Reese looked at her healed right arm and went wide-eyed.

"W-wow… Th-thank you so much! This means so much to me!"

Large tears of joy ran down her face, and she bowed repeatedly. Having a discolored wound like that had to be difficult for a teenage girl. I was glad I could heal it for her.

Looks like this darkness can even heal curses… I really hadn't expected it to heal the wound so easily. *Just what exactly is the Spirit Core that resides within me…?* I wondered.

"Master Allen, I also have a slash wound suffered during training…"

"Hey, wait your turn! Master Allen, I have an old injury as well. Could you please lend me your power?!"

A large group of girls crowded around me.

"H-huh… Hold on, I can't heal all of you at once!"

I spent the next little while using my darkness until I ran out of spirit power. In the process, I learned something new—the darkness was effective against any external wound. It healed anything instantaneously, from greater injuries such as lacerations, bruises, or curses, to lesser issues such as muscular pain, bad skin, or rashes. It had no effect on illnesses such as colds, however.

That week we spent our mornings in Soul Attire class, we ate lunch in a group of more than ten people, we did weight training in the afternoon, and we met up to train as we wished after school. The days were hard but fulfilling, and our last day at White Lily arrived in a flash.

"That is all for today's class. Please be careful on your way home," Kemmi said at the end of our final homeroom. I dashed out of the classroom as fast as I could as soon as she dismissed us.

"Hey, what the hell're you doing?!"

"Wait, Allen!"

Predictably, Shido and Idora raced after me with incredible speed. *Yeah, they're not gonna let me get away that easily...* I shot down a spiral staircase, flew out of the main school building...

"Stop running, Allen."

...and Idora used Flying Thunder to accelerate ahead and bar my way.

"Yeah, you're not getting away again."

Frigid air stabbed my back from behind.

"Ah-ha-ha... Looks like it..." I laughed bitterly, sighing internally.

"Come on, Allen. Let's do this," Idora said.

"This is our last day here. You can't put this off any longer," Shido threatened.

They both pointed their Soul Attires at me. They were itching for a fight. *They* really *want to spar with me...* Idora and Shido had been challenging me to a duel at every opportunity over the last two weeks. I had been coming up with excuses to put them off... But it didn't look like I would be able to get away this time.

It's not that I don't want to fight them... I was just worried that an all-out fight with Shido or Idora would lay waste to the academy. *Most importantly, fighting them would exhaust me and leave me unable to train for a period of days.* It would've been a waste to spend my valuable time at White Lily stuck in the infirmary. I had been avoiding their challenges for those reasons.

"*Haah*… Fine. I accept on the condition we forbid Soul Attires," I relented.

"Huh?"

"…No Soul Attires?"

Shido and Idora raised their eyebrows.

"That's right. If we use Soul Attire, I'll only be able to fight one of you today. I don't have unlimited spirit power."

"Tch."

"You have a point…"

"That's why I'm banning Soul Attires. That will let me fight both of you today… Besides, don't you think there's value in a bout of pure swordcraft?"

A duel with Soul Attires involved would undoubtedly turn into an intense, life-or-death battle. Such a situation would spell trouble for Shido, who lost control of himself once his temper flared. He would likely unleash Vanargand and cover White Lily in ice. That was why I'd proposed a duel without Soul Attires.

"Ha, that might be a fun change of pace. I'm in!" Shido said.

"I accept your terms as well!" Idora proclaimed.

That was how I came to duel Shido Jukurius and Idora Luksmaria without Soul Attires.

■

Shido and I followed Idora into a training hall. The Swordcraft Club was practicing there when we arrived, but they gave us the facility without argument when Idora explained the situation. The large crowd of girls from the Swordcraft Club watched us as Idora led me to the stone stage in the middle of the room.

"All right, Allen, we can fight as much as we want here!" she said excitedly.

Shido objected. "The hell do you think you're doing? Why do you get to go first?"

"I secured the location. The right naturally goes to me."

"What does that have to do with anything! Don't you remember how he just beat your ass in the Sword Master Festival? You should give up now. You don't stand a chance."

"Grr... And who was it who he squashed like an insect during the Elite Five Holy Festival?"

"Wanna repeat that?!"

...I had learned something over the last two weeks. Shido and Idora's belligerent personalities could not have been a worse match. *They're like oil and water...* I sighed just as the floor at Shido's feet froze and azure lightning began to flow through Idora's body.

Oh come on, do they have to do this now?! They would surely destroy this building if they fought here. That would defeat the purpose of dueling without Soul Attires.

"U-uhh... Oh yeah! How about we decide the order with Rock-Paper-Scissors?" I suggested after quickly jumping between them.

"Rock-Paper-Scissors? ...If you say so," Idora agreed.

"Whatever. Works for me," Shido accepted reluctantly.

"Okay, are you ready? Rock, paper, scissors...!"

I got them started, and they began to swing their hands down. I looked closely at their hands... and saw that Shido chose paper, and Idora chose rock. *I'm fighting Shido first.*

Shido laughed, and Idora's expression grew clouded. Powerful lightning then raced through her body. *Flying Thunder?! That's high voltage, too!* What in the world was she doing? I watched her hand closely and couldn't believe what I saw next.

O-oh my god! She calmly shifted her hand into a different shape. She had used her superhuman reflexes to see what Shido was going to do, and changed her pick just before she finished bringing her hand down.

""Shoot!""

Shido's choice remained paper, and Idora's hand formed scissors. Idora would be my first opponent.

"Ha, I win!"

She smiled boastfully, then took my hand and led me onto the stage.

That didn't feel fair... But I'd never said that Soul Attire wasn't allowed during Rock-Paper-Scissors. Idora also changed her choice while they were still lowering their hands. It may have been questionable ethically, but by the rules, she won.

"Hey, asshole! You cheated!" Shido shouted.

"All that matters is I won," Idora responded coolly.

"Grr..."

Shido was clearly unhappy, but he seemed to accept the result.

"A-anyway... Let's decide the rules before we start the duel!" I said cheerfully in an attempt to lighten the mood. "First of all, no using Soul Attire. Lethal attacks are also forbidden. As for the victory conditions... How about knocking your opponent off this stage?"

I based those simple rules on the Sword Fighting Festival, the Elite Five Holy Festival, and the Sword Master Festival.

"I have no objections. Let's get started!"

Unable to wait any longer, Idora drew two swords and assumed her unique stance. Her right foot was half a step forward, and her left foot half a step back. She practiced a two-blade style, so she held her right hand slightly high and her left hand drawn back behind her.

She slashes with her right hand and thrusts with her left. Her stance is as aggressive as ever... I braced myself and assumed the middle stance.

"Let's do this, Allen...!" Idora said.

"Yeah... Bring it on!" I responded.

Idora sprinted toward me.

"Thunderclap Style—Heavy Thunder!"

Her two swords cut through the air with lightning speed as she slashed at me ten times. I easily avoided the storm of slashes with my footwork.

...I can see it. Her gaze, her intentions, and her breathing were all

crystal clear to me. My long hours spent training every day looked like they were finally paying off.

"Grr, Thunderclap Style—Bolt from the Blue!"

Idora swung again without a moment's delay, but her seven lightning-quick slash attacks met nothing but air.

"No way..."

Her blades wavered for a brief moment as she widened her eyes in disbelief. Not letting that opportunity go to waste, I took a big step forward and unleashed a downward diagonal slash with all my weight behind it.

"*Hraagh!*"

"Ngh..."

Idora managed to block my blow by quickly crossing her own swords, but...

"Ahhh?!"

...She was unable to withstand the strength of my blow, and I sent her flying off the stage. That meant I had won the duel.

...That felt strange. It's like my senses have sharpened, or as if my power has further adapted itself to my body. This was just a hunch, but I didn't think it had anything to do with *his* darkness. I had a feeling there was a deeper, more fundamental *something* at work here. *I'll need to perform some tests later...*

Idora slowly climbed to her feet as I thought that over. "Allen, what was that absurd power? That's not humanly possible..."

"Hmm... I don't know...," I said, unsure of how to respond.

"Geez, way to lose in one hit. You really are pathetic... Stand back and watch how a true master fights, Idora," Shido said with a wicked grin. He swaggered onto the stage.

"...You shouldn't get cocky. Strength alone is not enough to beat him," Idora warned.

"Shut your trap... You think I can't see that?" He drew his blade.

I haven't fought Shido since the Elite Five Holy Festival... I felt slightly nostalgic as I studied his unique stance. He was standing upright with his sword dangling lazily in his right hand. His posture—which was the very picture of strength and composure—made it impossible to discern his center of gravity. Shido was a self-taught prodigy, which was how he'd developed his unique stance.

"Hope you're ready," he said.

"Come at me!" I responded.

We rushed toward each other simultaneously.

"Raaah!"

"Yaaah!"

Our blades collided violently, sending a blunt shock racing up my arms. I thought we were going to end up locking swords, but then Shido did something unexpected.

"You idiot!" he shouted.

"Huh?!" I gasped.

Just then, he slid his blade along mine with a perfect amount of force, stepping around my side with an elegant bit of footwork. *Th-that was really skilled!* He'd put force behind his sword at the exact right moment to catch me off guard, shifted his center of gravity fluidly, then stepped around me efficiently—he could not have executed the stealthy maneuver any better.

With the right side of my body defenseless, I made a split-second decision to jump far to my left. However, Shido employed his superhuman reflexes to prevent an easy escape.

"You're not getting away!" He matched my leap perfectly and swung his blade. "Take that!"

"Ngh…"

He sliced my right shoulder. Doing my best to endure the pain, I took a few steps back to put some distance between us. Fortunately, my wound wasn't deep. I was still in fighting shape.

"…You really are a prodigy, Shido."

"You half-asleep or something? You don't need to state the obvious."

"Ah-ha-ha, sorry."

I was amazed by Shido's intuition for combat. *His reflexes are super-human. It's like he's made of springs.* His incredible adaptability was his most impressive aspect. He'd completely switched up his fighting style after watching my last duel with Idora. Instead of relying solely on his immense arm and leg strength like he'd done during the Holy Festival, he was using a softer fighting style that took advantage of his speed and flexibility.

I can't get roped into fighting his preferred style. One of the fundamental rules of swordcraft was to steer the duels toward your strengths. I couldn't let Shido control the distance, not to mention the pace and rhythm of the bout. *I'll break him with my next attack!*

I kicked hard off the stage and closed in on him with a single step.

"Eighth Style—Eight-Span Crow!"

"Ha, that's weak!"

Shido defended himself perfectly by dodging or deflecting all eight slash attacks. However…

"I'm just getting started…!" I declared.

"Huh?!" Shido gasped.

…I took another large step forward and showered him with more swipes of my sword.

"Cherry Blossom Blade Secret Technique—Mirror Sakura Slash!"

Four mirrored slash attacks descended on Shido from the left and right, making eight in total.

"Goddamn it… Don't insult me!"

His reflexes kicked in, and he parried the slashes perfectly with incredible speed.

Shido really is good… It took a lot for me to create a chance to hit him. In deflecting the combined sixteen slashes of Eight-Span Crow and Mirror Sakura Slash, he'd momentarily left his torso open to attack. I kicked him as hard as I could.

"*Hraagh!*"

"Gah..."

My blow sent Shido flying hunched over through the air. He crashed into the wall of the training hall. He was clearly out of bounds, which meant I had won.

"Phew... I'm done," I said to myself. Having defeated both Idora and Shido, I used the darkness to heal the wound on my right shoulder and calmly sheathed my blade.

"H-hold it... *Haah, haah...* Don't even try to leave! We're gonna keep fighting until I win...!" Shido seethed, holding his stomach as he staggered to his feet.

"I want to keep going, too!" Idora declared. She had watched my match with Shido intently. It felt like I was going to be stuck here until they were satisfied.

"U-uhh... I don't know about that..."

I racked my brains over what to do, and the door to the training hall flew open.

"Hey, wait!"

"We can't let you hog Allen."

"Oh, my God! Would you deign to cross blades with me as well?!"

Lia, Rose, Cain, and the rest of the White Lily Class 1-A entered the building.

"Master Allen, could you please train us as well?"

"I want to experience your swordcraft firsthand!"

"This is our last day attending the same academy! Can we fight you, too?"

Shirley, Misha, and Reese bowed and spoke in unison.

""""Please...""""

The rest of Class 1-A followed suit. I may have been here for only two weeks, but I'd formed a bond with these students as we studied swordcraft together. There was no way I could refuse such fervent requests.

"...Okay. Let's make the most of our final day!"

I braced myself and decided to grant them all a duel. About an hour later...

"First Style—Flying Shadow!"

I sent a ranged slash attack toward Ries, who held her sword horizontally to defend herself.

"Ahh?!"

Her thin arms lacked the strength to stop it, though, and my projectile knocked the sword out of her hands. Victory was mine.

"Are you okay, Ries?"

I picked up her sword from the stage and handed it to her.

"Y-yes... Um... Thank you very much!"

Ries blushed for some reason and half ran from the stage.

She was my fiftieth opponent... I wiped a thin layer of sweat on my forehead and looked toward the line. *Looks like just over seventy more?* I was far from done here. *I'm getting kind of tired...*

I rolled my shoulders and took a deep breath as the next challenger took the stage.

"Hello, Allen Rodol. I'm a third-year, but do you mind if I fight you?"

She was a bear-sized girl—only slightly smaller than Ms. Paula—with short blond hair and tough, chiseled features. It was none other than Lily Gonzales, the student who had served as White Lily's captain in the Sword Master Festival.

"I don't mind, but... Go easy on me, okay?" I responded.

"Ha, don't be ridiculous. There's no way I can afford to slack off against you. I'm going to give you everything I've got." Lily lifted her enormous greatsword overhead. She had a twinkle in her eyes.

You've gotta be kidding me! I quickly drew my blade and assumed the middle stance. This unexpected opponent threw me for a loop, but... *I suppose I could consider myself lucky.* It wasn't every day you received the opportunity to fight a swordswoman as skilled as Lily. This was sure to be a great experience.

"Are you ready?" Lily asked.

"Any time!" I responded.

And thus my last day at White Lily Girls Academy turned into a grand event in which I sparred with over a hundred opponents.

■

I said goodbye to Shido, Cain, and everyone from White Lily after finishing the marathon of duels, then began my journey back to the Thousand Blade dorms with Lia and Rose. It was ten at night, well past sunset.

"Man, I'm exhausted...," I said, lifting my arms and stretching.

"I can't believe you just defeated a hundred opponents in a row...," Lia muttered.

"Technically, it was one hundred and twenty-three... That was truly astounding," Rose said.

"Ah ha-ha. Trust me, I'm more than a little sore."

Unsurprisingly, fighting one hundred and twenty-three duels in a row was a bit tough on me physically. Those duels were a kind of farewell party, though, and I had a great time. I was grateful that the White Lily students had sent me off with such grandeur.

"All right, it's back to training at Thousand Blade tomorrow!"

I slapped my cheeks to fire myself up for tomorrow.

"Hmm-hmm, oh Allen... Why do you get so excited when you talk about training?" Lia asked.

"I confess I can't quite match your enthusiasm," Rose said.

They both chuckled.

My everyday training at Thousand Blade would resume tomorrow. My Class 1-A classmates had likely gotten significantly stronger from their time at Ice King Academy. *I need to push myself even more to keep up!*

Feeling fulfilled by our brief transfer to White Lily Girls Academy, we returned to our lives at Thousand Blade Academy.

CHAPTER 2

The Senior Holy Knights & the Land of Sunshine

It was the first day after the end of my transfer period at White Lily Girls Academy.

"Ngh…"

I awoke to warm sunlight streaming in through the curtain. I drowsily checked the clock and saw that it was half past seven in the morning. There was still time before first period, but I needed to start getting ready.

"*Hraah…*"

I stretched wide and got out of bed.

Man… My body feels kind of heavy… It turned out that a single night of sleep wasn't enough to recover from fighting over a hundred people. *Guess I'll wash my face,* I thought as I left the bedroom.

"Oh, you're up. Good morning, Allen," Lia greeted me energetically. She looked even more cheerful than usual today. My fatigue lifted a bit at the sight of her.

"Good morning, Lia. Is that your winter uniform?" I asked.

I noticed that she was wearing a different outfit. Today was the first of October, which was when we were supposed to switch from our summer uniform to our winter uniform.

"Yeah… H-how do I look?" Lia asked me nervously after doing a little twirl.

She was wearing a short white dress that fit snugly on her body's curves under a warm red jacket accented with black. The beautiful contrast of white, red, and black really brought out Lia's stunning blond hair.

"It looks great on you," I said.

"Ha-ha, thanks. Oh, right. Show me how you look in your winter uniform."

"Sure, but… the male winter uniform doesn't look much different from the summer one."

"I still want to see it!"

I changed into my new outfit after Lia rushed me through my morning routine.

"…What do you think?" I asked.

Honestly, there was barely anything different about the male winter uniform compared to the summer uniform. It consisted of a white jacket accented with black and pants of the same color. The only difference was that the material had been cut thicker for cold weather.

"You look really cool!" Lia said with a radiant smile.

"Ah-ha-ha, thank you," I responded. I didn't think it looked much different, but…it must have looked good for her to be so complimentary. "Wanna get going?"

"Sure."

We decided to leave for class after we'd finished showing our uniforms to each other. I opened the door and felt a cool wind announce the arrival of autumn.

"It's kinda chilly… Are you cold?" I asked.

"No, I'm fine… It's finally starting to feel like fall," Lia responded.

I looked around and saw that the leaves on the trees were already turning yellow. We walked leisurely through the campus while basking in the changing of seasons, and the main school building of Thousand Blade Academy came into view. It was a nostalgic sight.

"Wow, it's totally back to normal!" I said.

"Construction technology in Liengard is truly incredible…," Lia commented.

Both the main school building, which my Spirit Core had completely destroyed, and the gymnasium, which the Black Organization had blown up, were totally back to normal. Even the interior of the main school building, which had been full of rubble two weeks ago, was mended entirely.

I sighed after we walked through the dust-free halls and stopped at the door to Class 1-A.

"I'm a little nervous," I said.

"Me too. We haven't seen everyone in two weeks… This is nerve-racking," Lia agreed.

"Okay… I'm opening the door."

"Do it."

Steeling myself, I pushed it open.

"Hey, long time no see, Allen!"

"Morning, guys! How've you been?"

"Hey, you two! Tell us about White Lily!"

My classmates all rushed toward us at once.

"*Hraah*… Mornin', Lia and Allen."

A moment later, a sleepy Rose walked through the door behind us. The entire class had now arrived. We spent the rest of the time until morning homeroom talking about our time as transfer students. Eventually the bell rang, and the classroom door flung open.

"Good morning, boys and girls!"

It was Chairwoman Reia, looking as cheerful as ever. She observed us closely and nodded with satisfaction.

"You all have toughened up in the short time since I last saw you! I can see it in your faces! It's morning homeroom, but…I don't have any important matters to discuss. Let's skip right ahead to first period!"

""""Yes, ma'am!"""""

And thus my normal life at Thousand Blade Academy resumed.

■

The next month passed without incident. Our mornings were occupied by Soul Attire class. I joined the Student Council for regular meetings at lunch. Our afternoons were filled with weight training and lectures. I spent my free time with the Practice-Swing Club. They were fulfilling days when I could devote all of my time to swordcraft.

One November day, the chairwoman summoned Lia, Rose, and me to her office. I opened the imposing black door to find Chairwoman Reia just finishing this week's issue of *Weekly Shonen Blade*.

"There you are. Sorry for calling you here so abruptly," she said, producing three papers from her desk and handing them to us.

Is this a résumé? I thought, puzzled.

"I summoned you three here for a very special reason. I am thinking of recommending you as senior holy knight special trainees."

"""…Special trainees?"""

None of us was sure what she meant.

"Oh, I suppose I shouldn't be surprised that you've never heard of that. The system was just implemented this year." The chairwoman cleared her throat and started to explain. "To keep it brief, the Holy Knights Association introduced a new system to recruit the top students from the Elite Five Academies. As you know, international relations are at an unprecedented level of instability. That's why the Holy Knights Association has implemented the Special Trainee Program to secure more capable personnel and better prepare themselves for any trouble that may arise."

She took a sip from her glass of ice water and continued.

"Participants in this program will be assigned to a holy knight branch on the weekends, where they'll undergo senior holy knight training and deepen their understanding of what it means to work as one."

"Interesting…," I responded.

This was an opportunity for students to work on their swordcraft by training with senior holy knights, and the Holy Knights Association was hoping to use this program to recruit promising young talent. It sounded like a mutually beneficial arrangement for the students and the holy knights.

"Joining this program will mean losing your weekends. Your days are going to be grueling. I'm not forcing you into this, but it will be a beneficial experience. I want you to give it some serious thought," the chairwoman finished.

I quietly shook my head. "I'm grateful, but… Unlike Lia and Rose, I can't produce my Soul Attire yet. I cannot accept this offer."

Being able to summon your Soul Attire was a requirement for senior holy knights. This rule was clearly stipulated, and there wasn't a single exception in their ranks. I politely refused the chairwoman's offer as I lamented the situation in my mind.

Haah… What a shame… I'd wasted an opportunity to achieve my dream of becoming a senior holy knight. *My Soul Attire gets in the way yet again…* When in the world would I obtain mine? I really resented my lack of talent.

"Oh, don't worry about small details like that. I'll clear things up with the Holy Knights Association myself," Chairwoman Reia said casually.

"R-really?!" I exclaimed.

"Ha, don't underestimate the influence of an Elite Five Academy chair. I may not look it, but I'm quite the big shot. Besides, how could they pass up a chance at Allen Rodol? They're going to be over the moon at the opportunity to obtain the greatest talent of this generation."

The chairwoman smiled kindly. I didn't hear much of what she said; I was too distracted by the joy welling up in my heart.

I-I did it… I did it, Mom! Becoming a senior holy knight would give me a stable monthly salary. That would allow me to give my mom, who'd raised me as a single parent and was still working hard in Goza Village every day, an easy life. The thought filled me with warmth.

"Allen appears to be on board… What about you two, Lia and Rose?" the chairwoman asked.

"I go where Allen goes," Lia said.

"Same here," Rose followed.

It sounded like they were going to join me.

"Great to hear. I'll contact the Holy Knights Association. Take those résumés to the Aurest branch at nine tomorrow morning."

"Yes, ma'am!"

"Got it."

"Roger that."

We left the chairwoman's office.

■

The next morning, Lia, Rose, and I went to the Aurest branch of the Holy Knights Association. We entered the large building, submitted our résumés at reception, and were led to the senior holy knights' training hall. It was as large as a gymnasium, filled with rows and rows of swordfighters wearing soft white coats.

There's so many people... They easily numbered over one hundred. According to the receptionist, the people in this hall were holy knights who had obtained their Soul Attires and were up for promotion to senior holy knight. They would receive the promotion if they passed today's practical exam.

"I'm getting kind of nervous...," Lia said.

"Tell me about it... It's so tense in here," Rose agreed.

They both gulped, intimidated by the peculiar atmosphere that tended to fill a room prior to a test.

"Anyway, let's go line up," I said.

"Yeah," Lia responded.

"Good idea," Rose said.

Thirty minutes passed as we waited. It was well past the scheduled start time of nine in the morning, and the room was growing restless.

"...They're not showing up," I said.

"I wonder what happened?" Lia responded.

"Maybe the proctor got hurt?" Rose speculated.

After another ten minutes of waiting, the inner doors of the training hall burst open.

"Hey, punks. I'm Instructor Don Golurg... Good grief, you all might be the dumbest-looking batch of candidates I've seen yet."

Don Golurg had a graying crew cut and his stern face was lined with black stubble. He stood at just over 180 centimeters tall and was as broad as a boulder. I guessed he was in his mid-fifties. He was wearing the same white coat as the other holy knights in the room. He reminded me of the teachers at Grand Swordcraft Academy.

He showed no remorse for how late he was as he scratched the back of his head and insulted everyone in the room.

"I need to start by looking at your boring-ass résumés. Swing your swords like the monkeys you are until I'm done," Instructor Don commanded.

""""Yes, sir!"""""

The holy knights responded briskly, but Lia and Rose looked offended.

"How dare he speak to us that way after showing up forty minutes late... Does he *want* me to burn him to a crisp?" Lia seethed.

"I'd be more than happy to feed him to my Winter Sakura," Rose growled threateningly.

"H-hey, calm down... How about we just do as he says?" I responded.

Our conduct would reflect on Chairwoman Reia. We couldn't cause an incident on the first day. I decided to calm them down and start performing practice swings as he instructed us to.

""""Hah! Yah! Hoh!"""""

I assumed the middle stance, raised my blade overhead, and swung it down. Everyone in the room performed the same action repeatedly. *This is way too stiff...* Swordcraft was supposed to be free and fun. Wielding your blade like this because someone had ordered you to was...wrong.

Holy knights began to drop out one by one after we passed the one-hour mark. By the two-hour mark, a decent number had given up. Their shoulders heaved, and large beads of sweat formed on their foreheads.

It hasn't even been three hours since we started swinging our swords... Are they sick or something? I grew worried about their health.

"Halt." The door burst open and Instructor Don walked in holding a bottle of alcohol. "I see some of you wimps have already given up... You're an embarrassment to the holy knights!" he yelled, kicking the stomach of a holy knight who was resting in the corner.

"Blargh?!"

"You losers will never be senior holy knights! Pack up your things and run home to your mommies!"

""""W-we're sorry...""""

The holy knights who'd stopped the exercise before the instructor returned left the training hall with regret on their faces. *I feel bad for them*, I thought.

"We have a poser in our midst!" Instructor Don shouted sternly. "Allen Rodol! Come forward immediately!"

"U-uh, yes sir!" I responded.

"Do you know what you've done, punk?"

"Um...I've been doing practice swings."

I couldn't think of anything else I had done since getting here.

"You dolt! Don't play dumb with me!" he yelled, shoving a piece of paper in my face. It was the résumé I had submitted at reception earlier. "Name: Allen Rodol. Education: Thousand Blade Academy. And what do you know—Soul Attire: Unrealized. What is the meaning of this?"

Instructor Don must have been angry about the fact I was here despite not having manifested my Soul Attire. That was strange; he should've already been notified of that.

"Um, Chairwoman Reia should have mentioned—"

"I don't want to hear your sorry excuses! A third-rate swordsman who can't even use his Soul Attire has no right to talk back to me!"

He ignored my attempt to explain myself. *Speaking to this guy is just going to be a waste of time.* Maybe it would be better to come back after consulting the chairwoman.

"…Very well. Please excuse me," I said. I made to leave, and Lia spoke up out of irritation.

"That's so unreasonable. You should listen to what Allen has to say—"

"Who gave you permission to speak?!"

"Huh?!"

The instructor struck Lia, knocking her off her feet.

"…Hey," I snapped. I felt a rush of anger and blanketed the entire training hall in darkness.

"Wha?!"

"Eeek?!"

"What is this?!"

"Where have I heard 'Allen Rodol' and 'darkness' before…? Hold on, isn't he that infamous young swordsman?!"

I ignored the comments from the peanut gallery as I stepped in front of Lia and thrust my mock black sword at the instructor. He raised his eyebrows and drew the blade at his back. I forced down the rage welling up inside me and made a proposal.

"How about a duel, Instructor Don?"

"A duel?"

"Yes, one-on-one. If I lose, I'll never show my face at the Holy Knights Association again. I'll leave right away."

"Hmm. And?"

"If you lose, you'll apologize to Lia on the spot."

"Pfft… Ga-ha-ha-ha-ha!" Instructor Don burst out laughing. I had no idea what he found so amusing. "You really are a moron. You already ruined your chance of ever becoming a senior holy knight the moment you pointed your sword at me. I'll never let the likes of you in! But I do enjoy a reckless challenge... I accept!"

He took off his white coat, revealing his muscular upper body.

"Haaaaaaaaa!" he yelled maliciously. It looked like his strength wasn't all talk. "Wa-ha-ha, it's time for my favorite hobby—beating the snot out of brats like you until they beg for mercy!"

"Sorry, but I don't plan on losing to a man who would shame the holy knights by hitting a woman."

That was how I came to duel Instructor Don Golurg of the Holy Knights Association.

■

Instructor Don looked around at the darkness enveloping the training hall after readying himself for combat.

"By the way... What is this strange darkness?" he asked.

"Don't worry about it. It's only my partially realized Soul Attire," I informed him, maintaining the middle stance.

"Pfft. So that's the best you can do? What a fitting power for a sorry swordsman like you!" He laughed mockingly. Then he gave a ferocious yell and sprinted toward me. "Yaaaaaaaa! Windy Mountain Style—Mountain Strike!"

He slammed down his sword from overhead. I coated my left arm in darkness and caught the blade.

"What the...?!"

The instructor widened his eyes in astonishment, but there should have been no cause for surprise.

"Can you give this duel the respect it deserves, Instructor?" I asked.

That was a sham of an attack. He hadn't been trying to knock me out or end the duel with it—he simply wanted to hurt and torment me. Genuine swordfighters like Shido and Idora would never stoop to using a move like that; they made their every blow in the interest of defeating their opponent.

"Duels between swordsmen are serious business. I'll cut you down if you don't give me your all next time," I warned, letting go of his blade.

"H-how dare you...!" Instructor Don jumped backward, his face flushed red with rage. "You're just some no-name brat... You'll pay for mocking me!"

He reached upward...

"Sharpen—Mountain Gale!"

...And pulled a copper sword from out of nowhere.

There it is. That was his Soul Attire—a piece of his Spirit Core manifested as a weapon. This was the power I was training nonstop to obtain.

"Ha-ha-ha! Jealous?" Instructor Don smirked as he showed off his Soul Attire. I ignored his provocation and studied his weapon.

That's wind and...sand. I strained my eyes and saw small grains of sand swirling around his longsword. It appeared as if his Soul Attire could manipulate two entirely different substances—wind and earth. I could see he hadn't become a senior holy knight instructor for nothing.

"Pfft... Want to know what always gets you Reject Swordsmen who can't use Soul Attire?" he said with a sadistic grin, lifting his longsword overhead.

"...What is it?" I asked.

"Simple...you've got no chance against all the long-range attacks these things can dish out! Sand Blast!"

The instructor swung his sword down and sent over twenty blades of sand rushing in my direction. His wind shot them forward as fast as arrows.

"You're right about that," I said.

Shido's Freezing Spear. Claude's Abio Troupe. Dodriel's Dark Shadow. Long-range attacks with multiple hits were what gave swordsmen without a Soul Attire trouble. Fortunately, I now had an answer for that.

"Dark Shadow."

My sharpened darkness cut down the approaching sand swords.

"Huh?!" the instructor shouted.

"There we go! That felt good," I said to myself.

Dark Shadow—an attack consisting of three masses of darkness—worked just as I thought it would. It was a new move that I'd created by referencing Dodriel's shadow powers. *Its range is about two meters. I'm still working on it, but...* Judging by its debut, the move would be more than enough to defend myself against multi-hit ranged attacks.

"Wh-what the hell was that?!" Instructor Don pointed at the blackness drifting in the air, wide-eyed with astonishment.

"I just told you, didn't I? It's my partially realized Soul Attire," I said briefly, shifting my center of gravity to my toes. "Prepare yourself."

"Grr... I can take out a halfwit like you in one swing!"

I kicked off the floor and charged toward him, getting in close enough to deliver a fatal blow.

"H-how are you so fast?!"

"*Hraagh!*"

I performed a downward diagonal slash aimed at the left side of his chest. He blocked it by whipping his sword around diagonally.

"What?!"

Despite his successful guard, I overpowered him and sent him flying backward.

"Ngh, how can someone so scrawny...be so strong?!"

Shock in his eyes, Instructor Don landed with surprising grace for his large body. I sent a projectile at him the moment he landed.

"First Style—Flying Shadow!"

"That won't work on me!"

He swung his blade hard to deflect the black Flying Shadow. I expected him to do that.

"I wasn't counting on it."

"Whuh?!"

I had hidden behind the Flying Shadow to easily close the distance between us. I didn't often use my First Style to inflict damage; I primarily deployed it as a trick to distract my opponent, restrain them, or give myself a chance to adjust our proximities to each other.

"Eighth Style—Eight-Span Crow!"

I brandished my mock ebon blade and unleashed eight slash attacks.

"Haaaaaah?!" The instructor swung his sword desperately and managed to deflect five of the slashes. "Gah…" The remaining three struck him on the right hand and both of his legs. "You pathetic Reject Swordsman…!"

Twisting his face in anguish, the instructor swung his longsword wide. I easily dodged by stepping back. *Those are some deep wounds.* There was no way he could keep fighting with his legs that banged up.

"I've won. Admit your defeat," I said casually, pointing my weapon at him.

"…outh," the instructor mumbled, looking down and trembling.

"…? I didn't catch that," I said.

"I said shut your mouth! You're not even half my age! How dare you act like you're better than me!" he yelled, stabbing his Soul Attire into the floor. "Sandstorm!"

A tempest swept up around Mountain Gale. The violent gale whipped up grains of sand so fast, they could kill on impact.

…What a pain. I used my sword to deflect the grains of sand flying in the air and looked around. The sand was scattering in all directions, breaking windows, tearing up the floorboards, and damaging anything it came into contact with.

"Geez, this sucks…," Lia said.

"I can't imagine anything more annoying!" Rose shouted.

They both drew their swords and skillfully deflected the grains of sand riding on the powerful winds.

"Owww…"

"Spare me!"

The holy knights had trouble warding off the particles, and they cried out in pain one after another.

"Ha-ha-ha! This is all that Reject Swordsman's fault for making me get serious! So blame him! This isn't even close to my full power! Sandstorm!"

The instructor bellowed and poured even more spirit power into his technique. The storm kicked up, blinding everyone in the room and leaving no opportunity to dodge the sand. *This really is irritating...* Seeing no other option, I summoned a great amount of darkness and wrapped Lia, Rose, and the rest of the holy knights in protective cloaks.

"Wh-what the...?!" Instructor Don shouted.

Everyone in the room survived Sandstorm unscathed.

"Judging by your reaction, I'm guessing that was your most powerful move?" I said.

His move summoned sand and wind to attack the area indiscriminately. I was sure it would have been very effective in a large-scale battle, but it didn't shine in a one-on-one bout.

"Th-this is ridiculous... How could I lose to this third-rate swordsman...?" He collapsed to the floor and appeared to lose consciousness.

"I win. Now apologize to Lia," I demanded, sheathing my sword.

"Wa-ha-ha, you'll regret lowering your guard! Windy Mountain Secret Technique—Landslide!"

C'mon... Sheathing my blade is hardly lowering my guard... I readied my fastest attack in response to his stupidity.

"Seventh Style—Draw Flash."

My sword glistened as I whipped it out of my scabbard to cut Mountain Gale clean in two.

"H-huh...?!"

Finally at a loss for words, Instructor Don fell to his knees. The training hall burst into applause.

"That polished swordcraft, overwhelming spirit power, and unmistakable darkness... There's no doubt about it! You're *the* Allen Rodol!"

"I-I was at the Sword Master Festival! You were so cool!"

"Can you please teach me the ways of the sword? ...And give me your autograph?!"

The holy knights rushed toward me with sparks in their eyes.

"Ah-ha-ha...I'll get back to you later..." I politely declined their requests and looked at the instructor, who was on his hands and knees.

"Impossible... This must be some kind of mistake... How could I have lost to some Reject Swordsman who can't even use his Soul Attire...? This can't be happening...," he muttered deliriously as he stared blankly at his broken Soul Attire. He was overcome with shock at having lost to an opponent he'd openly mocked moments earlier.

"Instructor Don Golurg, can you please acknowledge your defeat?" I asked again.

"Grk... I'm... sorry... Forgive me...," he forced out after grinding his teeth and clenching his fists.

I gave a loud sigh now that the duel was over. *Haah... What should I do now...* The training hall was decimated, the instructor was wounded, and I was unharmed. *How can I explain this to the Holy Knights Association...?*

One day with the holy knights was all it took to get roped into a stressful incident.

■

As I searched my brain to come up with an explanation for the ruined training hall, I heard footsteps coming toward the room. I figured a member of the Holy Knights Association was rushing here after hearing the windows break. *I'm just going to have to tell them what actually happened...* I didn't know if they would believe me, but I decided it would be best to tell them the truth.

A man walked into the training hall after I'd made up my mind.

"What was that sound... Huh?"

The man—who was wearing eccentric clothing that made him look

like a harlequin—stared openmouthed at the shocking state of the
training hall. An oppressive atmosphere befell the room.

"C-Clown...," one of the holy knights muttered.

He must be the branch manager, Clown Jester...

Clown Jester had long purple hair. He was thin and about 185 centimeters tall. I guessed he was in his early thirties. I couldn't decide if
his sharp eyes, gentle mouth, and shapely nose made him look kind or
cold. He had two conspicuous marks on his face—a red spade on his
right cheek and a black heart on his left. His unique attire resembled
that of a clown, and he was also wearing a fedora with a feather attached.

It wasn't good to judge people by their appearance...but this guy
looked seriously sketchy. I remembered Chairwoman Reia telling us
that a man named Clown Jester had assumed the position of branch
manager at the holy knights' Aurest branch a week ago.

"So... Would anyone be willing to fill me in here?" Clown asked with
an awkward smile. Stress showed on his face as he surveyed the ruined
training hall.

"Th that brat just went berserk out of nowhere!" Instructor Don
yelled, pointing at me.

"This boy here?" Clown asked, looking at me.

"Yeah, him! Be careful, Clown. Don't let his small stature fool you—
he has the strength of a demon!"

Lia and Rose immediately protested the instructor's nonsense.

"Hey, don't be ridiculous! You're the one who went berserk and
wrecked the training hall!" Lia yelled.

"You also struck first, remember?" Rose asked.

"Grr...," the instructor seethed. Outnumbered two to one, he glared
menacingly at the holy knights. "H-hey, back me up here! You all saw
what this brat did, right?! ...Right?!"

"""" """"
...

He was clearly threatening them. Overwhelmed, the holy knights all
held their tongues.

...I can't blame them for that. Instructor Don was their boss. There was no merit in disobeying a direct order to defend someone they had never met. *Now I'm at a disadvantage, though...* As terrible a person as Don Golurg was, he was an instructor here. Neither of us had proof beyond our testimony, and the branch manager would surely believe his subordinate over me.

What should I do...? I searched my brains for a way out of this situation.

"H-he's lying! Instructor Don is the one who wrecked this room!" a holy knight yelled loudly.

"Y-yeah, I saw it, too! The instructor lost his mind and laid waste to the training hall!"

"It's all Instructor Don's fault, Mr. Clown!"

The first holy knight to speak out had spurred others to reveal the truth as well.

"Y-you goddamn snakes...!" Instructor Don glared at the holy knights.

"Don, is this true?" Clown asked dispassionately. His expression was unreadable.

"Y-yes...it's true. But I didn't have a choice! This brat spoke back to me!"

"I see. By the way...is that bottle yours?"

"Hmm...? Yeah, why do you ask?

"Drinking on the job is forbidden per the Holy Knight Rules of Employment. I assume you're aware of that?"

The Holy Knight Rules of Employment provided employee guidelines for all holy knights around the world.

"Ha, what do I care about those stupid stipulations?! Do you realize how many decades I've been working here as an instructor? My rules are all that matter here! That's always been the case—ask all the previous branch managers!" Instructor Don ranted.

Clown shrugged. "Hmm... Understood. Don Golurg, you are fired—effective immediately."

"What did you say...?"

"I will send a notice of your dismissal to your home. Thank you for your extended service."

Clown removed his hat and bowed, then walked past Instructor Don as if he had nothing more to say.

"You think you can fire me one week after transferring here... I'll put you in your place! Sand Blast!"

The enraged instructor swung his broken Soul Attire and sent over twenty sand blades at Clown.

"Look out, Mr. Clown!" a holy knight yelled.

"...You really are thickheaded. Can't you tell how much stronger I am than you?" Clown said.

The sand swords crumbled, as if they'd hit an invisible wall. That wasn't all.

"Wh-what the hell?!" The instructor crouched as if he had been forced down to the floor. "Ngh... Oooooooooooh!" He looked like he was struggling desperately to get up, but he couldn't even lift a finger. A powerful force seemed to be keeping him down.

Is this gravity...? No, it's not. This mysterious power was affecting only the instructor. The damaged floor around him would have been creaking if it had been gravity. *The branch manager may look ridiculous, but he's really strong...*

Clown smiled casually despite the tension in the room. "You are interfering with the cleanup, Don. It's about time you leave." He released the man from the strange power. Instructor Don then glared at me.

"Goddammit... I'll make you pay, Allen Rodol!" he yelled, running out of the training hall.

"H-huh..." For some reason, he was only angry with me. I clearly didn't deserve it, but there was no point in complaining. *Haah... I hope he doesn't give me any more trouble.* I scratched my cheek.

"You're Allen Rodol, I presume? I've heard a lot about you. Welcome to the Aurest branch of the Holy Knights Association," Clown said, smiling kindly and offering his right hand.

"Thank you for the invitation, Mr. Clown," I responded. I took his hand and shared a friendly handshake.

"...Wow, you have nice hands." Clown narrowed his eyes, and he gave a satisfied nod. "I have a few things I'd like to discuss with you." He looked around the ruined training hall and smiled wryly. "But first... would you be so kind as to help me clean this place up?"

"Yes, of course," I said.

We grabbed brooms and dustpans and cleaned up the training hall with Clown.

■

Lia, Rose, and I gathered in the branch manager's office after we'd finished cleaning the training hall.

"Come on in. Make yourselves comfortable," Clown said, motioning toward a sofa in the middle of the room.

"Excuse us," I responded. We sat down on the sofa.

"Please, have some citrus water."

A woman set four glasses on the table in front of us. She was probably Clown's secretary.

"Thank you," I said. I was thirsty after three hours of practice swings, so I accepted it gladly. "...! This is really good!"

"Mmm! The aftertaste is so refreshing!" Lia exclaimed.

"Yeah. This is just what you need after a training session," Rose agreed.

Clown sat down on the sofa opposite us as we enjoyed the citrus water.

"Sorry about all that. We've given you a lot of trouble on your first day... The Holy Knights Association is rather old-fashioned, so we have to deal with a few people like Don," he apologized, the worry plain on his face. He seemed like a sensible person so far, despite his outlandish apparel.

"Please, don't worry about it," I responded, brushing aside talk of Don Golurg. Clown clapped his hands.

"All right—this is a little late, but allow me to introduce myself." He took off his fedora and bowed respectfully. "I am Clown Jester, the branch manager of the Aurest branch of the Holy Knights Association. I was just posted here a week ago, so I don't know this place much better than you! Nice to meet you!" he joked with a kind smile.

He was a tough nut to crack.

"I am Allen Rodol from Thousand Blade Academy. Nice to meet you, too."

"I'm Lia Vesteria. A pleasure to meet you."

"I'm Rose Valencia. I'm looking forward to working together."

Clown sighed loudly after we'd introduced ourselves. "This is quite the surprise. I didn't expect to receive such a celebrity... Thousand Blade sure is generous!"

"...Celebrity?" I repeated.

"I'm talking about you, Allen. You're the dark swordsman who defeated *the* Wonder Child at the Sword Master Festival. I doubt there's anyone in this country who isn't aware of you at this point..." He curled his lips into a grin. "I've heard a lot about you two as well, Lia and Rose. The Black and White Princess from Vesteria Kingdom, the Bounty Hunter who practices the Cherry Blossom Blade School of Swordcraft, and best of all, Allen Rodol... It's a thrill to have all three of you here."

Clown rubbed his hand together and said, "A thrill indeed." He sure was a flatterer.

"Anyway, I have a proposal for you all. Would you be interested in a foreign expedition?"

"What do you mean?"

"I'm asking if you want to go abroad and work as senior holy knights!"

"A-abroad?!"

"Ah-ha-ha, you won't be going anywhere too far. The location I'm considering takes no longer than two hours to reach by plane."

He was giving us an opportunity to travel to a foreign country. I would be lying if I said I wasn't interested. I would get to see the wider world with my own two eyes, visit new lands on my own two feet, and face strong new opponents with my own two hands. I had dreamed of having an experience like that for a long time. That being said, I couldn't neglect my classes at Thousand Blade.

"That's a very tempting offer, but we have our schoolwork to keep up with…," I responded.

"That won't be a concern. You're about to get a week off for fall break, right? That's the perfect amount of time for your first expedition!"

"Oh yeah…"

Clown was right—fall break would give us plenty of time to go abroad. Something was still bugging me, however.

"Um, why do you want us to go abroad so badly? Is there a problem with us training at the Aurest branch?" I asked.

His eyebrows twitched. "Good question… To be fully transparent, this branch is not worthy of you." A troubled expression came over Clown's face. "What I'm about to say is off-the-record. The senior holy knights here are rather lacking."

"R-really?"

"Yes. The best senior holy knights are working abroad, assigned to headquarters, or performing guard duty for the government. It pains me to admit this, but the holy knights at this branch—myself included— have a long way to go as swordfighters. It's a shame," Clown said, making an exaggerated frown. "So that's why I thought I would ask you about leaving the country! By the way, I'm planning on sending you to Daglio, the Land of Sunshine. It's a very peaceful country, which makes it perfect for your first expedition!"

"The Land of Sunshine, huh…" I looked at Lia and Rose. They nodded resolutely. It seemed like we were on the same page. "Understood. This is a great opportunity for us, so we accept your proposal."

"Wonderful! Let's spend the time until fall break getting you acquainted with the duties of senior holy knights! First off, would you go to reception and take a little lecture? It's a thirty-minute breakdown of the Holy Knight Rules of Employment and your chief duties," Clown said.

"Yes, sir."

Thus it was decided that we would spend our fall break working abroad as senior holy knights.

■

After watching Allen and the girls leave the branch manager's office, Clown's secretary asked a timid question.

"Um… Mr. Clown, was that really a good idea?"

"What're you talking about?" he responded.

"Daglio is a war-torn nation. The top-secret Operation Annihilation is about to begin. I think it's too dangerous there to send a group of students…"

"Ah-ha-ha, there's no need to worry about them. Allen is a Transcendent who overcame the curse of the 100-Million-Year Button, after all!"

■

We went from the branch manager's office to reception and listened to a thirty-minute lecture. It focused on two topics: the worker guidelines for holy knights and their chief duties. The Holy Knight Rules of Employment stipulated rules that all holy knights throughout the world had to abide by. The receptionist told us all about the moral code holy knights had to uphold, along with everything that was prohibited on the job.

Next she told us about the duties of holy knights. The Holy Knights Association was an international police organization whose mission was to ensure everlasting peace. To achieve this lofty goal, its members worked to maintain order and prevent crime, and they performed their various other duties with a strong sense of responsibility.

"That is the end of the general lecture. Thank you for listening. Please read this Holy Knight Manual for further detail when you return home," the receptionist said, handing us books so large, they could be used as weapons.

After the simple lecture, we began our special trainee activities by practicing with the senior holy knights and accompanying them on their patrols around the city. We were dismissed at seven in the evening and returned toward our Thousand Blade dorms.

"Hmm, that was a bit of a disappointment…," Lia complained.

"Yeah, the training was really easy… I feel like I barely even got a workout," Rose agreed.

They have a point. That wasn't nearly as intense as I expected… The practice swing session lasted only three hours, and the training after that felt lacking.

"We were probably right to agree to go abroad," I said.

"Yeah. Clown said the senior holy knights stationed in other countries are very skilled, so I'm sure it'll be a great experience!" Lia agreed.

"Ha, I'm getting excited," Rose said.

I decided to ask something that had been on my mind. "So we're going to Daglio, the Land of Sunshine. Do either of you know what kind of place it is?"

It was apparently a two-hour flight from Liengard, but this was the first I'd heard of it.

"Hmm, I can't say I know anything about it," Rose responded, putting a hand to her chin and shaking her head.

"Hmm," Lia began, seeming to sift through old memories. "If I recall correctly, Daglio is a small country to the southwest. I think it's a peaceful land that has declared permanent neutrality."

"You're so smart, Lia," I complimented.

"Hmm-hmm, thanks. What else…? I'm pretty sure Daglio is famous for its high-quality agriculture. They call their produce the 'blessings of the sun.' Their food is supposed to be delicious."

"…Wow, that's exciting."

My remote hometown of Goza Village didn't have much, but it sure wasn't lacking in agriculture. As a member of a farming community, I was proud of the crops we grew. The vegetables grown in Goza Village were fresh and nutritious as could be, the milk was rich, and the meat from our livestock was healthy and natural.

I wonder which tastes better, the produce grown in Goza Village or the "blessings of the sun" grown in Daglio...? I'll need to see for myself, I thought competitively.

"But...hmm," Lia said, tilting her head in anxious confusion.

"What's wrong?" I asked.

"Now that I think about it, I haven't seen anything related to Daglio in the news in years. That's weird. I learned everything I just told you from an old book I read when I was a kid."

Lia fell deep into thought, and Rose spoke casually. "It's probably just getting buried by bigger stories."

International relations were more unstable than ever. The Black Organization had been very active recently, and the Holy Ronelian Empire was puppeteering it from the shadows. The Five Powers were working to strengthen their relationships. The Holy Knights Association was sending skilled swordsmen all over the continent to keep the peace. There likely wasn't room in the newspaper for news on small countries.

"Oh yeah... You're probably right," Lia responded, her fears eased. Rose came to a stop.

"Here's my room. Good night, Allen and Lia," she said.

"Night, Rose," I responded.

"Good night, Rose," Lia said.

Lia and I returned to our dorm and slept peacefully in the same bed, like we always did.

■

The first day of fall break arrived a few days later. The three of us boarded an aircraft owned by the Aurest branch of the Holy Knights

Association and left Liengard. After a bumpy two-hour flight, we reached Daglio, the Land of Sunshine, to find a gentle rain.

"...It's drizzling," I observed.

"Yeah, this is some dreary weather...," Rose commented, looking up at the thick clouds covering the sky.

"H-huh... That's strange...," Lia mumbled, scratching her cheek. She seemed troubled by how wildly the current sight diverged from her knowledge of Daglio.

How did this happen? The ground was soft as clay, and the mountain in the distance was reddish-brown. It was obvious it hadn't just been raining for the last few days—it had been raining nonstop for a month, maybe even a year. The "Land of Rain" fit this place way more than a name like the "Land of Sunshine."

"Greetings, Allen, Lia, and Rose. I have been awaiting your arrival. Please, follow me," a local holy knight said.

He led us toward the building where the senior holy knights were residing. After a lengthy walk down a muddy road, we reached a large wooden house towering over the coast. It appeared as if they were using this place as their base of operations. We opened the large front doors and saw senior holy knights in white outfits.

"...Hm? Those are Thousand Blade uniforms... Oh! You must be the capable reinforcements we heard about!"

"Mr. Clown told us about you. He said you're the Black Fist's favorite students!"

"Tomorrow is finally the day of Operation Annihilation. We're counting on you three."

The senior holy knights gathered around us with expectant eyes.

"R-reinforcements? What do you mean?" I asked.

"I have a really bad feeling about this...," Lia said.

"Me too...," Rose agreed.

The holy knights' disturbing words left us confused. The room seemed strangely tense as well. A large man approached us from deeper into the room.

"Welcome to the temporary Daglio branch of the Holy Knights Association. I'm the interim branch manager, Ben Trioc. Nice to meet you!" he said in a deep voice.

Ben Trioc had a cleanly shaved head. He was about 185 centimeters tall and likely in his late thirties. There was an old scar on the right cheek of his chiseled face, his skin was tanned, and you could tell how muscular he was even through his uniform. He seemed intense.

"I'm Allen Rodol. It's a pleasure to meet you as well."

"I am Lia Vesteria. Nice to meet you."

"I'm Rose Valencia. Thank you for having us."

After sharing short self-introductions, I asked about the disturbing revelations we'd heard earlier. "Um, can I ask a question? What is Operation Annihilation?"

"Huh? Did Clown not tell you?" Ben asked.

"All he told us is that Daglio is a peaceful country…"

If I recalled correctly…

It's a peaceful nation, which makes it perfect for your first expedition!

I was pretty sure that was what he said.

"*Haah…* That's Clown for you…" Ben scratched his bald head. "Whatever. Unfortunately, the Land of Sunshine has become a war zone. 'Peaceful' couldn't be a less fitting description."

"""…Huh?"""

We all froze in disbelief.

"Daglio has been under the control of the Black Organization for the last few years… Not a day has gone by without fighting since their takeover."

"B-but I haven't heard any news about that at all!" Lia exclaimed, leaning forward. She sounded shocked.

No matter how small Daglio was, a country being conquered by the Black Organization was a big deal. This should have warranted a special edition of the newspaper.

"The Holy Knights Association and the Five Powers are restricting information on the matter. It's not surprising you haven't heard about this," Ben explained with a shrug. That was a bombshell.

"Th-they're restricting information…," I repeated.

"That was the correct measure to take. The world would fall into a panic if people learned that the Black Organization had seized an entire nation. This cannot become public knowledge."

He was right about that.

"I suppose I should fill you in on the situation. Daglio is in a pitiful state," Ben began with a serious expression. "A few years ago, the Black Organization invaded out of nowhere and conquered this place with overwhelming force. The Holy Knights Association realized the gravity of the situation and immediately dispatched senior holy knights to get it under control, but…the enemy's strength greatly surpassed our expectations. The first squadron of knights suffered devastating losses and had to retreat. The second and third squadrons of holy knights managed liberate thirty percent of the land to the south, but the remaining seventy percent to the north remains under the grip of the Black Organization."

Ben paused to shake his head.

"The villages' Black Organization rules are practically living hells. That band of villains subject the citizenry to heavy taxation and treat them like they're less than human. This is occurring as we speak…," he muttered.

Ben clenched his fists. His eyes were burning with rage. He seemed like a genuine, kindhearted person.

"It's been three years since the Holy Knights Association dispatched us, the fifth squadron… And upper management has finally given us the go-ahead to start Operation Annihilation. Our target is one of the Thirteen Oracle Knights residing in the royal castle located on Daglio's northern tip. The basic orders are to capture the enemy's stronghold and exterminate the remainders of their forces scattered throughout the country. It's nice and simple, just the way I like it! Right, you all?" Ben called out.

"Yeah!" the senior holy knights responded with deep voices.

Their morale seemed very high.

"What else is there to discuss…? Oh, right. According to the citizens we've rescued, this annoying rain has been pouring down on the Land of Sunshine ever since the day the Black Organization took over. It's likely the product of Soul Attire. And it takes great power to change the weather, which means it's almost certainly the work of that Oracle Knight," Ben finished sourly.

"Huh…"

Lia, Rose, and I were at a loss for words at the overwhelming amount of information we'd just learned.

"But, man, it sure is reassuring having you three here! With your strength, we'll kick the Black Organization's ass for sure!" Ben said, clapping me on the back.

They clearly weren't planning to let us go back to Liengard.

"Please don't get your hopes up too high…," I said.

I had definitely gotten stronger after training for over a billion years, but that was only in comparison to other students. I was a big fish in a small pond. Ben and the other senior holy knights worked throughout the world and were likely much more skilled than me.

"Ha-ha-ha, there's no need to be so humble! You're the Black Fist's favorite students, right? And Crazy Clown gave you his seal of approval, too. Plus, Allen even got the attention of the Blood Fox, Rize Dorhein! It's astonishing what you've accomplished at your age!" Ben laughed heartily. He was interrupted by a piercing siren. "Huh?! Excuse me for a moment!" He walked to the back of the room. "Has something happened?!"

A senior holy knight responded tensely, "A signal flare was spotted in Lao Village in the middle of the country! It was red—the Black Organization is attacking!"

"*Tch*… How large is the enemy force? Is the Oracle Knight present?!"

"Five black signal flares were sent up after the red one! That means the enemy numbers about fifty people! No sign of the Oracle Knight!"

"Got it! Holy knights, prepare for combat!"

""""Yes, sir!""""

The senior holy knights quickly got ready and entered formation.

"Allen, Lia, Rose, we're throwing you right into the fire! Show us what you can do ahead of tomorrow's Operation Annihilation! I'm counting on you!" Ben said, clapping me on the back again.

"Y-yes sir…"

After being sent into an intense war zone without our knowledge, we headed toward Lao Village with the senior holy knights.

■

Lao Village was a pastoral hamlet located in the center of the Land of Sunshine. It had once been peaceful, but that was now many years in the past. Today its residents suffered under the oppressive rule of the Black Organization, whose heavy taxes had brought poverty and famine. The exploitation had transformed it into a hellish place.

It was the monthly tax collection day. Beneath a simple tent without walls in the middle of town, the eighty-year-old mayor brought his forehead to the mud as he prostrated himself before a member of the Black Organization.

"This is all we have to offer… Will you please accept it?"

The mayor presented potatoes, rice, and a small amount of meat gathered from the village. It was truly all they could spare.

"Haah…" Zam Hashfelt—the man assigned to collect Lao Village's taxes—sighed loudly. "Oh, Mayor… You know screwin' with us is dangerous, right? I can tell at a glance this isn't enough."

"…"

The mayor gave no response. The Black Organization demanded ten tons of foodstuffs a month as tribute. The type of food offered didn't matter as long as they reached ten tons. That volume hadn't been an issue at first, given Daglio's agricultural output, but the situation had since changed dramatically. The rain had poured endlessly since the Black Organization conquered the country. A couple weeks of rain would have been manageable, but Daglio hadn't seen the sun once in years.

Two young men behind the mayor ground their teeth and put their foreheads to the mud as well.

Goddamn Black Organization…

They're the ones making it rain like this. They just want to make us suffer…

The never-ending rain had washed the fertile soil into the ocean, and the thick clouds blocked the sunlight. There was no way the villagers could match their usual output in these poor conditions. They had been doing their best to pay the taxes by growing crops indoors with artificial lighting, but they could no longer keep up.

"I understand that this is not ten tons… But it is impossible to grow sufficient crops in this environment. Our food stores are now empty, and malnutrition has caused an epidemic… This is truly all we can offer this month. I beg you, please accept it…," the mayor pleaded with his forehead still in the mud.

Zam smiled kindly and put a hand on the old man's shoulder.

"Hey, wanna know something? All we need from this island are the soul crystals you can mine here. Do you realize what that means?" he asked.

"Wh-what?" the mayor responded.

"It's simple, really. It means we couldn't care less if you live or die, or if you pay your taxes or don't… Hah!"

Zam drew his sword and swung it into the mayor's back.

"Gah…"

"M-Mayor?!"

"You bastard… Why would you do this?!"

The other two villagers raged. Zam grimaced in response.

"Goddammit, will you keep it down…! I've got a massive hangover…" He had a headache from spending the previous night chugging the alcohol he had collected. "I'm gettin' sick of gathering taxes like this every month… Killing you all would be much more fun."

The great number of swordsmen behind Zam all drew their swords.

"Sh-shit…!"

The two young men pulled wooden flutes out of their pockets and played loudly for the whole village to hear.

"Didn't I just tell you to shut up?!" Zam yelled, slashing the men with his blade.

"Argh…"

"Crap…"

They fell to the ground just as red and black signal flares shot into the sky from the north of the village.

"Hmm… Those signal flares. Probably a distress call for the holy knight rats down to the south. Ha, how pathetic," Zam sneered. "All right guys, let's enjoy some hunting before those wannabe heroes show up!"

""""YES, SIR!""""

That was how the tragedy of Lao Village began.

■

Katarina Garrish and her five-year-old daughter, Mireille Garrish, grew frightened in their old house in southern Lao Village as the alarm sounded and the signal flares went up.

"Th-that sound…"

"Mama…?"

Mireille looked at her mom with unease, and Katarina hugged her tight. She would protect her daughter, no matter what. That was the final promise she made to her husband before the epidemic had claimed his life half a year ago.

"It's okay, Mireille. There's no need to worry. I'm here," Katarina said.

"O-okay...," she responded.

Katarina calmed her daughter down, then cracked a window to peek outside.

"My word..."

She saw the mayor and two men collapsed and bloodied in the center of the village. Deciding they needed to skip town immediately, Katarina grabbed a sword for self-defense out of a cabinet. *We should reach a holy knight station if we head directly south...* Katarina tried to come up with a route they could use to escape undetected and gently grabbed Mireille by the hand.

"Mireille. Bad people are attacking the village. We're going to escape to the holy knight station since it's so dangerous here. You have to stay quiet on the way, okay?"

"O-okay..."

Katarina led Mireille out the back door.

"Oh, dear... Where are you two sneaking off to?"

They ran straight into Zam Hashelt, the man from the Black Organization who Katarina had just seen attack the mayor. Her plan had already fallen apart.

"..."

"M-Mama..."

Fear showed on Katarina and Mireille's faces.

"Heh-heh-heh, look at the terror in your eyes... I love it! There's nothing better than this!"

Zam loved a good hunt. He found much more joy in tormenting the weak as they tried to escape than he did in killing capable fighters who opposed him. That was why he'd rushed to the south of the village after killing the mayor and the two men. He'd predicted that the women, children, and elderly would attempt to flee to the holy knight station directly to the south of Lao Village.

"...Mireille, leave me and run," Katarina commanded.

"B-but…," she protested.

"I'll be fine. Just focus on running south. You can't turn around no matter what." Katarina pushed her daughter in the back.

"I-I don't wanna… Come with me, Mama…," the girl requested, shaking her head. Tears welled up in her eyes.

"Don't worry about me. I'll catch up as soon as I can. Remember the promise you made to Daddy? You told him you would be strong… Or am I misremembering?"

"O-okay…"

Mireille nodded, and they heard grating laughter and obnoxious applause.

"Pfft… Ah-ha-ha-ha-ha! I'm so moved! It's like you're *trying* to make people cry! I'm gonna relish killing you!"

Zam smiled wickedly and drew his sword.

"I won't let you reach my daughter, even if I have to give up my own life to stop you!" Katarina declared, awkwardly grabbing the shabby blade at her back.

"Oh, you're a swordswoman…" Zam stiffened for a moment, but his cruel smile returned once he noticed how crudely she held her sword. Katarina was struggling to hold the middle stance, the most elementary of positions in swordcraft, leaving herself vulnerable. She was clearly no match for him.

"…Run, Mireille!" Katarina shouted.

"O-okay…"

Mireille began to flee after hearing her mom's shriek, only to stop a few seconds later when she got a bad feeling. It was quiet—too quiet. She heard no swords or screams. The only sound was the patter of the heavy rain. Finding that strange, she slowly turned around.

"Ma…ma…?"

When she did, she saw something unspeakable—her mom, with a sword plunged through her chest.

"Heh-heh-heh… Ah-ha-ha-ha-ha!" Zam cackled loudly as the rain fell on him. "Nothing beats murder, am I right?!" Katarina's blood was splattered over his face and clothes. He took a moment to savor the kill, then wrenched sword out of Katarina's chest and turned to his next target. "Aren't you going to run, little girl? This scary man is going to slice you a new one!"

"..."

Mireille stood rooted to the spot, overcome with fear and despair. "N-no... Mama..." She began to weep.

"Aww, that must have been so scary... Don't worry, it'll all be okay. I'm about to reunite you with your precious mama!" Zam yelled, raising his sword excitedly.

"Not...so fast..."

Despite having been stabbed in the heart, Katarina somehow grabbed Zam's arms from behind.

"Wh-what the hell? You're still alive?!" he shouted.

The woman's eyes were bloodshot, and he grasped on to her with impossible strength. Zam flinched at the ferocity of her instinct to protect her child.

"Run... Mireille...!"

"..."

Even as her dying mom told her to run, Mireille couldn't move. She shouldn't be blamed for that—this horrible situation was too much for a five-year-old girl to process.

"W-will you die already... I stabbed you through the heart!"

After returning to his senses, Zam shoved Katarina off and stabbed her three more times.

"Mi...reille..."

Her final promise to her husband had been to protect their daughter. Having given her all to achieve that, Katarina collapsed slowly to the ground.

"Geez, that had to have hurt like hell. And for what, just to save a few seconds? I'll never understand parents...," Zam said with a shrug. He let the rain wash the blood off his sword. "All right, little girl, time for you to join your mama in the afterlife. You don't want her to be alone, do you?"

"N-no... Stay back...," Mireille pleaded. She slid away backward from the slowly approaching Zam. Her moist eyes, the exhaustion on her face, and her desperate desire to escape gave him a sadistic thrill.

"Heh-heh-heh... Woo, hunting is so much fun!" He smiled wide and lifted his sword overhead. "Give me your best scream!" He mercilessly swung down his blade, which had taken so many lives.

Mama... I'm sorry... Mireille shut her eyes tight—and an ebon slash attack flew past her.

"...?!"

Zam twisted instinctively and managed to dodge it. A moment later, a boy armored in darkness jumped between the two of them. He had distinctive black and white hair. The boy spoke kindly to Mireille.

"I'm know that was scary, but everything's okay now. I'll put an end to this."

As soon as he had finished speaking, repulsive darkness flooded out of his body and covered Lao Village in an abyss of black.

■

After reaching Lao Village, I held the mock black sword in the middle stance and looked at the thug before me.

"...Why do you all do such horrible things?" I asked to buy time. *It's not too late... I can still save them!* The darkness could heal even mortal wounds. As long as the target was alive, it could heal any injury in seconds. I summoned a massive amount of spirit power and blanketed the village in darkness, covering the injured in black cloaks.

"Why, you ask? Hmm... I'm not sure how to answer that. It's a pointless question—you don't need a reason to kill someone. If I had to give one, though...I do it 'cause it's fun," the man answered.

"I see... That's an even more despicable motivation than I expected."

I'd succeeded at buying enough time to secure all the villagers with darkness. That ought to heal everyone who was still alive. I breathed a sigh of relief, and the man gave me a friendly smile.

"So, kid. How are you gonna make up for interfering with my hunt? Die!"

The kindness on his face twisted to rage in an instant, and he slammed down his sword with intent to kill. I lightly swung my mock ebon blade in response to sever his like it was nothing.

"Wh-what the hell?!"

His eyes opened with shock, and I kicked at his vulnerable right flank.

"*Tch*, nice try!"

He quickly drew in his right arm and tried to block with his elbow.

"H-how are you so strong?!"

My darkness-enhanced kick powered through his attempt to defend himself and sent him flying like a ball.

"Bah, grah…"

After colliding with the ground multiple times, he sat up slowly, covered in mud.

"*Haah, haah… Shit…* Hey, help me out here! This guy's stupid strong!" he yelled.

"Heh, where is he?"

"What, you mean this kid? Give me a break, man."

"Ooo, this boy's kinda cute…!"

Three swordsmen in black clothing approached us.

"Be careful, you idiots! You wouldn't believe how strong this brat is… Let's summon our Soul Attires and attack him from all sides!" the initial man said.

They formed up around me with sharp gazes. After a short moment of silence…

"Secure—Thousand Vice!"

"March Free—Reckless Army!"

"Drown—Twisted Love!"

"Fall—Holey Land!"

...They summoned their Soul Attires and attacked me simultaneously. I muttered calmly in response.

"Dark Shadow."

A storm of sharpened blackness swept up around me.

"What the hell?!"

"Ha, ha-ha, you can't be serious..."

"Ooo, how wicked..."

"He's a monster..."

I engulfed the men in an abyssal darkness. They collapsed to the ground after I released them, their Soul Attires shattered. They were still breathing—I'd used only a fraction of my power.

All right, time to take out the rest. I dashed about the village, knocking out the remaining invaders as I did so. "Sweet, that's everyone." I calmly sheathed my sword once I had defeated the last one.

Lia and Rose showed up shortly afterward.

"Allen, are you okay?!" Lia exclaimed.

"You're way too fast! Where's the enemy?!" Rose demanded.

They both drew their blade and looked around alertly. Their foreheads were covered in beads of sweat.

"You can relax. I've already finished off all the Black Organization members here," I responded.

"G-guess I shouldn't be surprised..."

"You say the craziest things so casually..."

The senior holy knights arrived next. Ben widened his eyes in disbelief upon seeing the fifty unconscious swordsmen.

"Holy crap... Did you do all this by yourself, Allen?" he asked.

"Yeah. It wasn't too bad, fortunately," I responded. I'd been able to take out the swordsmen without any difficulty, but it would have been a different story had there been anyone as strong as the Oracle Knight Fuu Ludoras or Dodriel present.

"Y-you're good... I can't believe you killed them all without any help..."

"...Huh?" I responded, shocked by what Ben had said. "I didn't kill anyone."

"...What?" he said, dumbfounded. He reached down and felt the neck of a nearby swordsman. "...He has a pulse. You actually left them all alive?!"

"O-of course I did! It's not so easy for me to take someone's life!" I said, somewhat offended. Ben fell silent for some reason.

He was able to spare all of their lives while outnumbered fifty-to-one?! Is this guy even human?!

Ben gulped and laughed dryly. "Ha, ha-ha... I can see why Black Fist and Crazy Clown recommended you. To think you're still a student... I can't imagine how strong you're going to become."

"Uh, thank you...?" I responded absentmindedly. I wasn't sure what the sudden praise was for.

"Anyway... That was amazing, Allen! All right, everyone, tie up those Black Organization members! Don't let any of them go off by themselves. We're gonna squeeze them for every drop of information we can get!"

""""Yes, sir!""""

The senior holy knights tied up the arms and legs of the captured criminals with practiced hands.

"Allen, look over there!" Lia yelled suddenly, pointing. The girl I saved earlier was pressing a blade against an unconscious man. "We have to stop her!"

"...No, I don't think there's anything to worry about," I responded.

Though there was undoubtedly strong hatred in the girl's eyes, I could see warmth and kindness housed within them as well.

"Y-you'll pay for killing Mama...!"

She lifted the sword high, only to tremble and collapse, dropping the weapon.

"Th-thank goodness…" Lia sighed with relief. I walked toward the girl. "Allen…?"

"I'll be right back," I said.

I walked loudly so as not to surprise the girl and crouched to meet her eyes.

"Are you okay?" I asked nicely. She looked up with a face wet from tears.

"I couldn't do it… He killed Mama, but… But I was too scared… I-I couldn't stop shaking…" She did her best to respond to me in between sniffles.

"What's your name?"

"…Mireille."

"That's a pretty name. You're really strong, Mireille."

"…Huh?"

"It's not that you couldn't do it. You *chose* not to do it. You decided not to go down the same evil path as that man. You were strong enough to prevent your emotions from getting the better of you… Anyway, I have a surprise for you."

I snapped my fingers exaggeratedly to remove the cloaks of darkness protecting the villagers.

"…What did you do?" she asked.

"I used a little spell. Look over there," I said, pointing at Mireille's mom, who was breathing steadily.

"H-huh…?!" Mireille widened her eyes, and she ran as fast as her legs could carry her. "Mama! Mama! Can you hear me?!" She grabbed her mom's shoulders and shook them.

"…Huh? Where am I?"

The girl's mother slowly opened her eyes and sat up. It was as if she had never been injured.

"Mama!"

"…Mireille? O-oh yeah, where is the Black Organization?!"

She hugged her daughter tight and scanned the area.

"It's all okay now! This boy beat all the bad guys up! Then he used the most amazing spell ever and healed you!"

"H-huh... But my wound was so deep...how in the world did you heal it?!" Mireille's mom asked me in disbelief.

"Um..." I'd really been hoping she wouldn't ask me that. To be honest, I myself didn't understand the power I'd used to heal her. That was the truth, but telling her as much would have come across as suspicious. ...*Guess I've got no choice.* I decided to tell a white lie. "I...actually have a healing Soul Attire."

I figured claiming it was a healing Soul Attire would put her more at ease than if I said it was mysterious power I didn't understand.

"Wow... You must be famous if you can instantly pull someone back from the brink of death," she said.

"Um, yeah... Something like that." I couldn't just tell her that I'd lied... I felt a pang of guilt and looked away.

"You saved the lives of both me and my daughter... Thank you so much..." Mireille's mom bowed repeatedly.

"No need to thank me. I'm glad you're both unharmed," I responded.

"Hey, you got a second?" Ben said after tapping me on the shoulder.

"What's wrong?"

"Oh, nothing. I was just thinking we need to alter our strategy for tomorrow."

"Alter how...?"

I assumed he was referring to the strategy for tomorrow's operation to root out the Black Organization. I had no idea what kind of change he was considering—actually, I hadn't heard anything about the plan at all—but this felt very sudden.

"Let me start by saying I didn't necessarily doubt your strength. I just had no idea you had such a powerful healing Soul Attire, and you pair it with *monstrous* close combat skills. I've decided I need to adjust our strategy to make you the center of the operation. Will you lend us your might?" Ben asked.

"U-uh, yes sir...," I responded.

I wasn't even using Soul Attire, though... It sounded like I would need to set him straight.

■

After we moved to an inn in Lao Village, I explained the power of my darkness to Ben in great detail.

"Huh... I can't believe that ability isn't even your Soul Attire... You really are special, Allen," Ben muttered in disbelief, scratching his bald head. "That's a very unusual power you've got. I've seen hundreds of Soul Attires, but I've never come across one that can control darkness..."

"Really?" I asked.

"That darkness is so powerful, you even have me jealous! Use it well!"

"Thank you, I will."

A loud knock came at the door.

"Come in," Ben said, and a holy knight with a menacing, unshaven face entered the room.

"I have a report! The citizens of Lao Village are all safe and sound!" he declared.

"That's great!"

Miraculously, no one had lost their life. My darkness must have saved them in time. I was really glad to hear that. *This healing ability is insane...* I honestly didn't think I would be able to save Mireille's mom. I'd seen her get stabbed through the chest three times, and she could have very well been injured before that. I couldn't believe that I'd healed her completely from all that in just a few seconds.

...There's no doubt about it. The darkness is rapidly growing in power. I was glad for that, but it was also a little scary. Strange changes had been happening to my body lately. Some of my hair had gone white. My body got tougher every time I sustained an injury. My physical abilities increased limitlessly as I continued to train.

Oh no... I'm not starting to look like him, *am I?* My Spirit Core's hair was pure white, his skin was tough enough to deflect a knife, and his physical abilities were stunning. It seemed like we were only growing more and more similar over time. *Should I be worried about this...?* I wasn't going to wake up to find my body stolen, was I? I sure hoped that wasn't going to happen.

The menacing holy knight continued his report as those frightening possibilities crossed my mind.

"We got some new information out of the Black Organization members we captured! It sounds like the purpose behind their occupation is to mine the soul crystals found in this country!"

Soul crystals were a rare mineral found only in a few select regions. They were used to make the soul-crystal swords we wielded in class, and the Black Organization utilized them in the production of soul-crystal pills.

"We also got them to confess the identity of their leader, who conquered Daglio's royal castle—it's Raine Grad, one of the Thirteen Oracle Knights! The Black Organization calls him the Rainbringer, and he's supposed to be a fearsomely strong swordsman!"

Raine Grad. Another of the Thirteen Oracle Knights, huh... *That puts him on the same level as Fuu Ludoras, the man who attacked Thousand Blade. There's no doubt he's much stronger than me...* This was sure to be an intense battle beyond imagination.

"Hmm, I see...," Ben muttered after quietly listening to the report. Then he spoke up enthusiastically. "All right! Time to share our new strategy for tomorrow's decisive battle! Call all the senior holy knights to this inn!"

After that, we discussed Ben's New Operation Annihilation until we all knew it by heart. Then we headed to the royal castle to remove Raine Grad the next day.

■

The royal castle of Daglio towered over its surroundings on the northernmost tip of the country. Constructed of white brick, it looked more like a church than a fortress. Raine Grad—one of the Thirteen Oracle Knights, and the castle's new lord—sat with his eyes closed in silence upon a faded throne. The only noise that registered in his ears was the patter of endless rain. He might as well have been a statue as the seconds, minutes, and hours passed.

His silence was interrupted by hurried footsteps entering the throne room.

"L-Lord Raine!" yelled a man, a grunt for the Black Organization wearing a black overcoat.

"...What?" Raine responded, opening an eye. He was slightly irritated that his quiet time had been broken.

"The senior holy knights are rushing northwards! It appears they're serious about retaking Daglio this time!" the grunt gushed breathlessly, trying to convey the severity of the situation.

"...And?" Raine replied coldly.

"O-our front line has already collapsed... We are incapable of holding them back. Our forces in Dino Village and Rondo Village fled at the first sight of the enemy... Lord Raine, please lend us your power!" the man pleaded.

The grunt had no other choice but to plead. Raine had essentially conquered Daglio single-handedly. Without the enormous strength of one of the Thirteen Oracle Knights to aid them, the Black Organization members would have no hope of holding off the skilled senior holy knights.

"I will not," Raine refused. His tone brooked no argument.

"Wh-why?!" the man asked. Raine sighed in response to his persistence.

"*Haah*... Answer me this. How have you treated the people who came to you for help over the last few years?"

"U-um..."

"You tormented and killed them all, correct? You have never once even lent an ear to a plea for mercy."

"..."

"Fools, all of you. How selfish are you to expect you deserve any different?" Raine's angry voice echoed throughout the throne room.

"...What should we do, then?"

"I don't care. Whatever happens to you filthy lowlifes is none of my concern."

"But—"

"Enough. I am not leaving this castle. You all can flee if you wish," Raine said definitively. He closed his eyes as if to show he had nothing left to say.

The grunt finally lost his patience. "F-fine! I'll do it, then!"

"..."

Raine was motionless in his silence.

"You're definitely strong. Insanely strong. But these guys are too much for you! *The* Allen Rodol is with them! You know, the S-class threat who defeated Fuu Ludoras?! To make matters worse, he's also got Lia Vesteria, the host of the eidolon Fafnir, and Rose Valencia, the sole successor of the Cherry Blossom Blade School of Swordcraft with him! And don't forget Ben Trioc! They're all out-of-this-world powerful! You don't stand a chance in hell against them!"

The grunt yelled, "I hope they tear you to shreds!" before he sprinted away.

Raine mumbled to himself after silence returned to the throne room. "...More killing." He stared into space with an expression of grief and gave a self-deprecating laugh. "Ha, what am I hesitating for..."

He put his head in his hands and reflected on what he had done in Daglio.

"How shameful... I'm even more pathetic than those Black Organization thugs... Why am I feeling guilt now after all this time?" he lamented in the empty throne room. "So an S-class threat and the host of the eidolon Fafnir are on the way. This will all be over once I capture them… And then, the quiet land of Daglio will finally be a paradise just for the two of us…!"

Raine continued his solitary pursuit of his own brand of justice.

■

We raced north after leaving Lao Village. Though we passed through many villages under the rule of the Black Organization on the way there, the occupying members fled as soon as they saw us for some reason. That let us save time and get to our destination without expending much energy.

…*It's enormous.* Before us towered the Daglio royal castle. The white-brick building looked more like an old cathedral than anything else. The walls were covered in cracks and rotten ivy; it had clearly been a long time since they received any maintenance.

"Onward!"

""""Yes, sir!""""

The senior holy knights opened the large front doors at Ben's command. We walked through long, candlelit hallways and eventually emerged in a large hall that resembled an old chapel. The sooty crimson carpet, the crumbled pews, and the evenly spaced golden candlesticks lent the place a tranquil atmosphere.

On the other end of the room stood a man who dominated the space. He gazed at us with hollow eyes from atop a faded throne. "Welcome, uninvited guests." His deep voice echoed throughout the room.

Ben responded. "Are you the Oracle Knight named Raine Grad?"

"That I am," the large man answered curtly.

Raine Grad had long, dark blue hair tied behind his back. I couldn't tell exactly how tall he was because he was sitting down, but I figured he was close to two meters in height. He was in his late thirties. His hollow eyes, defined nose, pursed lips, and the short beard gave him a dark and cold look. He wore fine blue clothes under a black overcoat embroidered with a blue crest I had seen somewhere before. The worn-out gray scarf at his neck looked overly large and awkward.

Raine looked left and right before his gaze landed on me. "...I see. You're Allen Rodol, the boy the organization has designated as an S-class threat. You certainly do stand out from the rest." He guessed my name right away. The Black Organization must have circulated information about my appearance to its members. "Is that Lia Vesteria next to you?"

Lia and I gulped. It was intimidating being targeted by a large international criminal organization that was disturbing world peace.

"An S-class threat and an eidolon... That should be sufficient," Raine muttered cryptically before calmly rising to his feet. "Allen, Lia... Will you make a deal with me?" He walked toward us.

"A deal...?" I asked.

"...We'll hear you out, at least," Lia responded.

We encouraged him to continue while staying poised to draw our swords at any moment.

"If you two give yourselves to me, I'll let all the holy knights in this room go free... Not a bad deal, no?"

""Huh?!""

There was no way we could agree to that.

"Ha-ha-ha! I didn't expect you to be a comedian, Raine!" Ben laughed loudly and took a step forward.

"I am not joking. I'm just...tired... I don't want any more needless killing. Can't you see you are but insects before me? You have no chance, no matter how great your numbers."

I detected no lie in his voice. He was being completely sincere. *Raine's really sure of himself.* He seemed to believe one hundred senior holy knights were no match for him.

"Heh, you might wanna get those eyes checked. I'll teach you not to underestimate the holy knights!" Ben yelled, veins bulging on his forehead. He drew his blade. "Sow—Tree Seed!" He summoned his Soul

Attire to draw Raine's attention, and the rest of us began our surprise-attack operation.

"Conquer—Dragon King Fafnir!"

"Blossom—Winter Sakura!"

"Melt—Acid Staff!"

Everyone summoned their Soul Attires at once and surrounded Raine.

"Dark Box!"

I unleashed my darkness and wrapped Raine inside it. Everyone else sprang to action.

"Supreme Dragon Breath!"

"Sakura Blizzard!"

"Acid Ocean!"

Lia, Rose, and the senior holy knights produced all the spirit power they could muster and performed their most powerful long-range techniques.

All right, we did it! Dark Box completely cut off light and sound to whoever was trapped inside it; Raine would be robbed of vision and hearing as one hundred people hit him with everything they had. He may have been one of the Thirteen Oracle Knights, but he was going to have a very hard time enduring that without getting hurt.

But that expectation was betrayed…

"Erode—Eternity Drop."

…when a chill ran down my back. *What is this feeling?!* I had no way of knowing what Raine was trying to do inside Dark Box, but my instincts was sounding the alarm. *We're going to be in trouble if I don't do something…* Thinking that, I made the call to release the Dark Box.

"Wh-what are you doing, Allen?!" Ben exclaimed, startled by my deviation from the plan.

"Thousand Drops."

Clear arrows of water blanketed our vision. Each projectile housed shocking strength and easily blocked all of our long-range attacks before they continued toward us without slowing.

"That's impossible!"

"What the?!"

"This guy's insane..."

Everyone froze in shock.

"Come oooooooooooon!"

As the only one who saw this coming, I summoned a large amount of spirit power and covered all my allies in cloaks of darkness.

"...Impressive," Raine said.

I managed to save everyone in the nick of time.

"I-I survived...?" I heard someone's voice echo loudly.

"Th-that was close...," Lia said.

"We would've died if not for Allen's darkness...," Rose uttered.

They both went pale.

"Thanks, Allen. You saved us...," Ben said, sweating.

"*Haah, haah*... I'm just glad you're okay...," I responded. I had to catch my breath after using so much spirit power at once.

"Allen Rodol. You really are different from the rest," Raine said, holding his Soul Attire, which was shaped like a long tachi.

That was how my battle with Raine Grad, one of the Thirteen Oracle Knights, began.

■

We quickly transitioned to our next gambit after the surprise attack failed. Lia, Rose, Ben, and the other senior holy knights formed a large circle, leaving me and Raine at the center.

"...Let's do this, Raine!" I exclaimed.

"Bring it on," he responded.

I clad myself in dense darkness and dashed toward him with my sword sheathed. I was going up against one of the Thirteen Oracle

Knights; I couldn't afford to wait and see what he would do. *I can't worry about pacing myself. I'm going all-out from the start!*

I got in close enough to perform a powerful blow and unleashed my fastest draw strike.

"Seventh Style—Draw Flash!"

I accelerated my sword in its scabbard and slashed at Raine with tremendous speed. *All right, I got him!* Raine stared absentmindedly as my slash approached his side. It must have been too fast for him to react to it.

"Huh, not bad." Raine bent slightly to easily evade the attack.

What?! He was able to dodge from this close?! I was speechless at how fast his large body could move.

"It's my turn… Hrngh!"

Raine raised his tachi overhead and swung it down with all his might. *Now!* Shifting my weight down, I brought my sword around horizontally to block his blow. "Ngh, aaaaaaaaaah!" An enormous shockwave sped through my body from my arms to my feet. *I stopped it, though…* His physical advantage was evident, but he hadn't outclassed me in strength.

"Hmm. You're wiry, but powerful enough. Is there a secret to that strange darkness of yours?" Raine remarked, his eyes wide. I bet he never would've imagined that I would block his blow straight on.

"Like I'd tell you… Hah!" I moved left to slide his sword away and followed up with a no-holds-barred chain attack. "Eighth Style—Eight-Span Crow!"

"Nice move." Raine smiled fiendishly and defended himself with frighteningly perfect fundamentals.

H-he's so skilled… This guy didn't get into the Oracle Knights on strength and Soul Attire alone. Raine's defensive technique was as captivating as a ritualistic dance. That kind of skill couldn't be obtained in a day; it required decades of repetitive, tedious training to achieve.

"My turn." Raine leaned in and took a huge step forward…

"Hegemonic Style—Hard Strike!"

"Cherry Blossom Blade Style—Night Sakura!"

"Flower Garden Style—Field of Flowers!"

…only for Lia, Rose, and Ben to attack him together.

"Tch…"

Raine dodged some of the slashes, parried others, and blocked the rest, ultimately avoiding every last move…

"Huh… You grazed me."

…or so it had seemed. A drop of blood trickled down his cheek. Not even Raine could completely dodge a surprise attack from three elite swordfighters.

"…I see. You challenged me to a one-on-one duel so that the insects could strike when I wasn't paying attention. Not bad…," he said, complimenting our strategy. "I must say, you've surprised me, Allen. To think you can cross blades with me at your age…"

"…You sure look relaxed. Don't you realize the situation you're in?" I asked.

A numbers advantage made a huge difference in battle. We clearly had the upper hand.

"You're right that this isn't ideal," Raine responded, rubbing his chin. "I suppose I have no choice but to increase my numbers… Mimic Drop."

Two silver droplets fell from the tip of his tachi to the floor. They morphed in shape until they became copies of Raine, each as large as the man himself.

""""Huh?!"""""

We were all flabbergasted. *He can create copies of himself?!* Now that I hadn't seen coming. The eerie silver Raines stood on either side of the real one.

"This makes it three-on-one hundred. You still have the numbers advantage, unfortunately." He shrugged exaggeratedly, looking totally at ease.

"...That's a really strange ability," I observed.

"I could say the same for you. Your darkness is wholly unique." Raine snapped his fingers. "...Kill them."

The two copies rushed toward my allies.

Crap... I repressed my feelings of impatience and focused on the original Raine. *Trying to support Lia, Rose, and the holy knights would be a bad move.* That would allow Raine to do whatever he wanted and open up even more people to getting hurt. There was only one thing I could do here: hold him back myself.

...It'll be okay. Lia and Rose are strong. Ben and the others are senior holy knights skilled enough to be sent abroad to Daglio. I'm sure they'll defeat the copies in no time. Putting my concern for my friends aside, I focused on the opponent before me.

"Do you not tire of ordinary swordplay, Allen?" Raine asked.

"...What do you mean?" I asked.

"I was just thinking of giving you a greater taste of my power...Aqua Robe." Raine quickly ran his hand along the blade of his Soul Attire, coating it in a thin layer of water. It seemed like a meager change. "I'll give you one warning: Whatever you do, don't try to block my blade."

"Huh?"

"I suppose a demonstration is in order," he said. He ran his water-covered sword along the floor, leaving behind a deep gash.

"Huh?!" I exclaimed. His tachi was sharp enough to cut through the hard floor like butter. It was impossibly sharp.

"I have covered the blade of my Soul Attire, Eternal Drop, in high-pressure water compressed by a tremendous amount of spirit power. Your cheap sword cannot possibly block it, no matter how the darkness has strengthened it," Raine explained.

"...Thanks for the warning," I responded.

Raine cracked his neck. "Time for round two."

"...Bring it!" I yelled.

Raine quickly forced me into a defensive battle. I had lost the support of my allies and couldn't block his powerful strikes. I couldn't even give him a proper duel.

"Hrngh!"

"..."

I dodged his slash by a paper-thin margin and jumped back to create some space. But as our sorry excuse for a duel continued, I started to worry about something else.

"...Hey, Raine. Why do you look so miserable?" I asked.

"Excuse me?" he responded.

"I was just curious. I've never seen someone brandish their sword with such pain."

He had looked miserable ever since our fight began. Anguish filled his face regardless of whether he had the upper hand or not. *He's definitely hiding something.* I saw clear hesitation in his blade.

"What has you so—"

"You shouldn't pry into other people's business."

"Huh?!"

He delivered a furious kick to my stomach.

"Gah?!"

The blow knocked the air out of my lungs and sent me flying into the castle wall.

Fast doesn't even begin to describe him... I hadn't even been able to see that attack; before I knew what hit me, I was already winded. *He was going easy on me before, wasn't he...* Raine was even faster than Fuu Ludoras.

"Th-this isn't over..."

I got up slowly and assumed the middle stance, but my vision was blurry from the last blow. *Damn it, I need to keep it together...* I bit my lower lip softly to rouse myself. Then right after regaining my senses, I noticed something—the clangs of blades clashing against one another had all but disappeared.

Keeping Raine in the corner of my eye, I hesitantly looked around and found a nightmare. *You can't be serious…* Only Lia, Rose, and Ben were still fighting. The rest of the senior holy knights had been wiped out.

Crap, how did this happen…? The copies must have been much stronger than I'd pegged them for. *Should we run?!* We had no hope of winning as things stood now. Our opponent was one of the Thirteen Oracle Knights, a member of the Black Organization's senior leadership, after all. He was one of the greatest swordsmen in the world, whose strength rivaled an entire nation's army.

I can't do it. A student like me can't beat him one-on-one. That could not have been more obvious. *But how can we escape?!* There were nearly one hundred unconscious holy knights in the hall. It looked like they were just barely clinging to life, but they would be slaughtered if we ran now. Besides, I doubted Raine would let us get away in the first place.

Argh, what should I do…? This couldn't have gone worse. I tried my hardest to think of a way out of this…

"Ahh?!"

…and heard Lia scream behind me. I turned around to see Fafnir flying through the air.

"N-no…," gasped a now-defenseless Lia as one of Raine's copies turned toward her and swung down its tachi.

"Lia…!" Rose yelled. She hurried toward her, but she wouldn't make it in time.

Shoot… I summoned as much of my drained spirit power as I could and created a thick shield of darkness. It raced across the ground with tremendous speed to block the copy's blade just in time.

…Thank goodness, I thought, but my relief lasted only a moment.

"Do you really think you can afford to protect your friends while fighting me?" came a chilling voice behind me.

"…?!"

I reflexively turned around and saw Raine, sword overhead.

"Hrngh!" he grunted.

I flicked my blade horizontally to block his extremely fast downward diagonal slash, but that was the worst mistake I could have made. *Oh no!* I had spent over a billion years mastering my defensive technique; it was a hard habit to break after I'd spent so long hammering it in.

"I warned you about blocking me."

"Gah…"

Raine sliced the mock black sword in two and gouged into my chest with a fierce slash.

""Allen…?!""

Lia and Rose's screams sounded far away.

This is bad… I need to heal… I couldn't fight with a wound this deep. I immediately focused darkness onto my chest and started to heal myself. *Crap, it isn't healing fast enough…* The gash in my chest wouldn't close. I must have been nearly out of spirit power.

That was not surprising. It had been out of necessity, but I'd used way too much spirit power over the last two days. I'd fought fifty Black Organization members and healed the injured in Lao Village the day before, and today I'd wrapped all my allies in cloaks of darkness to protect them from Raine, then engaged him in an intense duel that required my maximum strength. It was actually impressive my spirit power had lasted this long.

But I can't afford to collapse yet… Out of breath, I summoned all my energy and forced myself to stand. I tightly gripped what was left of my sword and faced Raine.

"…According to reports, Allen Rodol's Spirit Core goes berserk when the boy is inflicted with a mortal wound…," Raine muttered to himself with a hand on his chin. "It's been about two months since Fuu Ludoras's failed mission… Not even an eidolon-class Spirit Core should be able to surface after that short a time. In fact, it is precisely because of its great power that it should not yet be able to emerge. I highly doubt his spirit power will be able to heal him quickly enough… But I might as well be careful."

Raine raised his tachi high and thrust it into the floor, summoning a large set of doors behind me. *What is that?* They were floating black double doors about five meters tall with an ominous pattern drawn on the front. Just looking at them filled me with dread.

I maintained the middle stance while remaining wary of the strange doors and Raine.

"Colossal Doors," Raine muttered. The doors opened slowly, and out rushed a swarm of hands made of clear water. There numbered well over one hundred, and they blanketed my vision.

This is another ominous move… I faced the incoming water hands and swung my damaged blade as hard as I could.

"Eighth Style—Eight-Span Crow!"

The branching eight slash attacks easily tore the liquid hands apart. *Those were surprisingly fragile…,* I thought, but the water quickly reformed a moment later.

"Huh?!" Over one hundred hands wrapped themselves around me and started to drag me toward the door. "Damn it, what is this technique?!" I quickly swung my sword to try to clear them away, and Raine spoke.

"Hm, it appears our fight has come to an end."

He was looking at Lia and Rose, who were both being held under the arm by one of his copies.

"Lia?! Rose?!" I shouted.

"A-Allen… I'm sorry…" Lia said.

"…S-sorry," Rose said.

They were both beaten up, and their limbs were bound by a mercury-like substance.

"Damn you, Raine…," I cursed.

"Relax. I am not going to kill them…yet," he responded.

In other words, he would kill them eventually. *I can't let that happen…* Now truly angry, I summoned the rest of my spirit power.

"Haaaaa*arraaaagh!* Dark Shadow!"

I produced incredibly sharp streaks of darkness to cut the water hands to pieces, but it didn't accomplish anything. I might as well have tried to stand a sword into a lake. No matter how I sliced at the hands, they always reformed and grabbed me again.

"Give it up, Allen. No one has ever escaped from this sealing technique. Just relax. The Colossal Doors only seal the target's consciousness—you will awaken in the next life having suffered no pain," Raine said.

"I'll never give up!" I shouted back. I used the last of my strength to resist as hard as I could, but I was unable to escape as the hands dragged me slowly through the doors.

Goddammit… There has to be something I can do! Lia and Rose were unconscious, and Ben and the senior holy knights had been long since incapacitated. Chairwoman Reia wasn't here. And most importantly, *he* was currently unable to emerge. It was up to me to find a way out of this pinch.

I thought as hard as I possibly could and landed on one very unlikely possibility. *This is a big gamble…* We would all die if I failed. *But it's the only way I can see out of this hopeless situation…*

I steeled myself and closed my eyes, then sank deep into the depths of my consciousness until I hit the bottom of my soul. When I entered the Soul World…

"Yo, I've been expectin' you."

…*He* was standing there wearing a malicious grin, true black sword in hand. He seemed to know about our predicament—that would save me some time.

"Have you found your resolve this time, punk?" he asked.

"I believe so," I responded. I nodded and drew my sword.

"Hmm. Good. This may be pointless when we already know how this will end, but…gimme all you got!"

He readied the ebon blade intimidatingly.

"…"

I felt such overwhelming malice from him that it made me want to run. Doing my best to keep my bearings, I quietly assumed the middle posture.

I've always swung my sword for myself. I practiced to improve my swordcraft, to become stronger, and to achieve my dream of becoming a senior holy knight. But that wasn't good enough. My resolve was lacking. I had no chance of defeating him unless I found a stronger drive.

I'm going to protect Lia, Rose, Mireille, and everyone else in this country! I'm going to use my sword to create a world where everyone can be happy!

I imprinted that firm resolve onto my heart and collected my breath.

"Ha, I like that fire in your eyes… You've actually gotten a little tougher," he said.

"There's no time to chat… Are you ready?" I asked.

"Yeah. I'm going to beat the hell outta you!"

I had the mock black blade. He had its true counterpart. We gripped our weapons and charged simultaneously.

"Haaaaaaraaaagh!"

"*Raaaaaaaaaargh!*"

I didn't need to think about distance, tempo, feints, or other intricacies of swordcraft when fighting him. It was just a pure test of strength.

I will… defeat him…! I was going to defeat him for myself, and more importantly, for everyone else!

"*Hraaah!*"

"*Raagh!*"

Our blades crossed and a momentary silence befell us.

"Oww..."

He slashed his sword deep into my chest as he passed me. *I can't... collapse yet...* I swallowed blood and slowly turned around.

"Well, there ya go."

He stood unhurt with a grin on his face.

"Damn it..."

I'd put everything I had into that attack, but it wasn't enough. I had worked so hard. So damn hard. I'd done my best to grow. But it still wasn't good enough. There was no way a Reject Swordsman like me could save anyone.

...Damn it all. My vision wavered as strength left my body. *Lia, Rose... I'm so sorry. I think this is it for me...*

My consciousness began to drift away...

"The brat's actually grown a little..."

...And then I noticed that the black sword in his hands had been broken clean in two.

Wh-what's happening...?

The next moment, a torrent of tremendous power rushed into my body. *Wow... What is this?!* The wound on my chest healed immediately, and a sinister darkness gushed from my body.

"A-are you sure about this...?" I asked.

I still hadn't defeated him. Was it really okay for me to borrow his strength?

"What nonsense are you spewin' now? You just broke my black sword, weak as you are. Cheer up, will you?" he responded.

"I couldn't defeat you, though..."

"Don't tell me... Were you actually trying to *win* that fight?"

"O-of course I was!"

No one would enter a duel intending to lose. I really had been trying to defeat him.

"Pfft... Gwa-ha-ha-ha-ha-ha-ha!" He burst out laughing. "Don't get a big head, punk! Try again after another hundred million years of training!" he yelled ferociously. My comment seemed to have really upset him.

"Well, anyway… Thank you."

I could fight with this power. I could use it to protect everyone.

"…Hmph, do your worst," he said, turning his back to me and returning to his usual spot atop the cracked boulder.

"See you later," I responded.

Having obtained tremendous power, I closed my eyes and returned to the real world—to my fight with Raine Grad.

■

The black doors shut tight after Allen was dragged through.

"…Allen?"

"No way…"

Lia and Rose's voices echoed vainly in the quiet throne room.

"Your Allen is gone. His consciousness has been sealed in darkness forevermore, never to wake again," Raine said casually. His expression was unreadable.

"Allen… I'm so sorry…"

"I'm sorry… We failed you…"

Lia and Rose apologized again and again. Allen had needed to protect them constantly. Not only were they not able to help him, but they'd also actively held him back. The two girls were both overcome with regret.

Guilt washed over Raine as he beheld their pain. *It had to be done. I didn't have a choice…* He ground his teeth and told himself that over and over again, trying to justify his actions to himself.

The truth was that Raine had never killed anyone with his own hands. The only sin he had committed since arriving in Daglio was using his Soul Attire, Eternal Drop, to summon the endless rain. The heavy taxes levied on the villages, the violence against the villagers, and the murder of Daglio's king had all been carried out of the grunts' own accord. There had been little Raine could do but overlook their repulsive actions. He would never achieve his dream if he openly opposed the Black Organization. That would render his joining the organization pointless.

"*Haah...*"

His guilt threatening to overwhelm him, Raine sighed loudly and shook his head. *Don't think about it. I've achieved my quota. Daglio is now all mine!*

Steeling himself, he looked at the bound Lia and Rose.

"My orders were to capture the eidolon Fafnir, regardless of whether the host lives or dies...," Raine said to himself. "It's your turn—Colossal Doors."

Raine poured more spirit power into the tachi pierced into the floor and summoned two new large black doors. They opened slowly, and clear water hands grabbed Lia and Rose.

"This will allow you to die painlessly, at least."

Raine believed he was doing them a kindness. As one of the Thirteen Oracle Knights, was well aware how inhumanely the mad scientists in the Black Organization treated their subjects. Lia Vesteria was a precious eidolon host and Rose Valencia was the sole inheritor of the Cherry Blossom Blade School of Swordcraft, which was once said to be the greatest school of swordcraft in the world. There was no way those curious scientists would pass up a chance to study them. The girls would meet a miserable end in a lab after having their bodies relentlessly poked and prodded. Raine decided it would be better to seal their consciousnesses here than to let them suffer in that way.

The water hands dragged Lia and Rose toward the doors.

"" ...""

They didn't resist. The mercury-like substance binding their limbs would have prevented them from struggling anyway, but even then, their guilt at holding Allen back robbed them of the willpower to struggle.

"...Sorry, Allen," Lia muttered.

Just then, an ear-splitting boom sounded, and a dreadful darkness smothered the throne room.

"What the?!" Raine shouted. The broken remains of the destroyed Colossal Doors clattered at his feet. A cold sweat ran down his back, and he gave an exceptionally loud gulp. *Could this power be...? No, that's impossible! His mind should have been completely sealed! No one has ever broken the Colossal Doors before!*

Raine slowly turned around to find Allen, unhurt and clad in wicked, violent darkness.

""A-Allen?!""

Lia and Rose's eyes lit up with hope.

"Sorry for worrying you two," Allen said. He smiled kindly as the blackness rushed toward the Colossal Doors that were trying to seal the girls. It devoured the doors like a ravenous predator, wiping them from existence.

"Th-this can't be!" Raine shouted as he watched the doors get swallowed whole before his eyes. This sealing technique had never once failed. He was shocked speechless.

Allen retrieved Lia and Rose with lightning speed and cut off the mercury binding their limbs.

"Thank goodness you're okay, Allen... I'm so relieved..." Lia leaped into Allen's chest, crying tears of joy.

"I'm glad you're okay, too, Lia." Allen hugged her gently.

"Are you really all right, Allen?!" Rose asked, patting him.

"Yeah. It's a long story, but I'm fine now," Allen responded, and stood up. "Sorry to ask this, but can you two step back? I doubt I have perfect control of this yet."

"Have you finally done it, Allen?!" Lia exclaimed.

"G-got it...," Rose said.

They both leaped backward after inferring what he was about to do. Once he saw that they were far enough away, Allen faced Raine unarmed.

"Sorry to keep you waiting," he quipped.

"...Allen, just what are you?" Raine asked while switching to a defensive position with his weight shifted behind him.

"I don't know what to tell you... I'm just an ordinary Reject Swordsman," Allen answered.

"...I see. I'll ask a different question, then. What did you do inside the Colossal Doors? How did you change so much in such a short amount of time?!"

Raine was an elite swordsman. He could tell at a glance that something was different about Allen.

"We would be here all day if I gave you the full story, but... You're right, I did go through one major change," Allen said. He raised his right hand into the air, and the room was overwhelmed with an intense pressure.

"..."

Raine gripped his tachi tightly as the sensation stabbed his skin. In that tense atmosphere, Allen finally unleashed his long-coveted power.

"Destroy—Insatiable Demon Zeon!" he yelled.

The true ebon sword appeared through a rift in the air. Its blade, hilt, and guard were all pitch-black. It was Allen's Soul Attire, the ultimate sword he had struggled so desperately to obtain.

So this is Soul Attire..., Allen thought. He gripped the ebon blade, and a storm of darkness erupted around him.

"Huh?!" Raine exclaimed.

"Ahh?!" Lia screamed.

"Wh-what is this...?" Rose gasped.

They all stumbled as the raging blackness spread throughout the room.

I suppose this is why the organization labeled him an S-class threat..., Raine thought. You would never know from his kind face that he possessed such repulsive darkness. It was wicked, abnormal, and enormously powerful. Raine braced himself like never before.

"Time for round three, Raine," Allen said.

"Yes… Show me what you've got, Allen Rodol!" Raine responded.

Allen Rodol faced Raine Grad with his newly acquired Soul Attire in hand, ready for another intense fight.

■

I gripped Zeon and locked eyes with Raine.

All right, what should I do? I didn't have total control over this power yet. I didn't even know where to start. *It's best to use Soul Attire in battle after becoming familiar with it…* Unfortunately, I didn't have that luxury. I was being thrown into the fire, but I could try to catch up by performing a few tests.

I'll try a simple attack first! I swung the black sword lightly to perform the move I used to restrain opponents.

"First Style—Flying Shadow!"

A projectile slash so large, it filled my field of view tore up the floor as it raced toward Raine.

""Huh?!""

He and I were both astonished.

Th-that's huge! *It looks like Dark Boom, but even bigger!* The technique's power far surpassed my expectations, leaving me at a loss for words.

"You're wasting no time showing me your full strength… But let's see you deal with this—Thousand Drops!"

Raine swung his sword and fired a thousand water arrows to intercept my attack. But Flying Shadow consumed the projectiles and continued on its path toward Raine.

"Wha… Hrrraagh!"

He then swept his tachi horizontally to barely deflect it. I was dumbfounded by what I had seen.

A-amazing… Flying Shadow isn't just a small trick anymore—it's an extremely powerful attack!

"Haah, haah… You have a lot of nerve hiding this level of strength until now, Allen," Raine muttered in annoyance. Sweat had formed on his forehead.

"I wasn't hiding anything. I only just realized this power now," I responded.

"Just now... Do you mean to say you obtained your Soul Attire while sealed within the Colossal Doors?!"

"That's right."

"Huh... Your mental fortitude is truly inhuman." Raine smiled bitterly then lifted his tachi—still covered in high-pressure water—above his head and leaned forward. "You are certainly strong, Allen. I can see why the organization declared you an S-class threat."

"Thanks."

"But no matter how powerful you are, you will not defeat me! You have not faced death as many times as I have! Your resolve cannot hope to match mine! And most importantly, you haven't spent nearly as much time honing your swordcraft as I have!" Raine yelled.

He entered striking distance with one large step.

"Guardian Soul Style—Water Tachi!"

A slash attack composed of clear water branched out in four directions and homed in on my neck, torso, and legs.

"I've spent a lot of time with the blade as well," I responded. Over one billion years of it. "Eighth Style—Eight-Span Crow!" My eight slashes of darkness painted the four water slashes black and cut Raine deep.

"Gwah..."

Injured, Raine jumped back far to collect himself.

"*Haah, haah*... Your fundamentals...are impeccable as well...," he panted.

"Well...fundamentals were all I had."

Back in my days as the Reject Swordsman, I'd had nothing to rely on but books. The training I knew of was practicing the fundamentals described in those texts, such as the middle posture, practice swings, and basic defensive techniques. I'd created a self-taught style after over a billion years repeating the foundations of swordcraft.

I studied Raine's body as we talked. *He's so toned...* My last attack had torn his clothes, and now his steel-like muscles were on full view. His wound wasn't deep—his muscles must have protected him.

Raine assumed the middle stance after catching his breath, and a blue pill fell from his pocket. *I recognize that color. That's a soul-crystal pill...* I remembered Dodriel telling me once that taking one of these pills healed all of your injuries in exchange for a piece of your lifespan. *It would be frustrating if he healed himself right after I finally managed to nick him.*

I'd heard that Soul Attires could only be used for a limited amount of time. *I have no idea how long Zeon will last. I don't want this fight to drag out.* I calmly waited for Raine to try to pick up the pill.

"...What foolishness," Raine said, before crushing it underfoot.

"Huh?!" I gasped.

"Why are you so surprised? Did you really think I would rely on a drug made by the scumbags in the Black Organization?"

There was clear disgust on Raine's face as he insulted the very group he belonged to.

"Why did you join them, then?" I asked. He worked for the Black Organization despite resenting them. That didn't make any sense to me.

"...There are things that are unobtainable unless you change your position. You will come to understand that someday, Allen," he responded with a mixed expression.

"...I see."

Zach Bombard—a member of the Black Organization who kidnapped Lia—had told me something similar. He claimed to have reasons for leaving the Holy Knights Association and joining the Black Organization.

"I admire your resolve, Allen," Raine said, drawing me back from memory lane.

"Huh?"

"Your swordcraft is straightforward and earnest—beautiful, even. I am sure you are in the right, and I am in the wrong..." He sounded like he didn't know what to believe himself. "However—just as you have your sense of justice, I have mine! I will not budge on that!" he yelled loudly, brandishing his sword with bloodshot eyes.

"Hrngh!"

"Hah!"

Our blades collided, setting off an intense duel. I succeeded in inflicting slash wound after slash wound.

"Ngh... This isn't overrrrr!"

Raine vigorously swung his sword down from his shoulder, and I responded with the same move. Sparks flew as our blades locked.

"Oooooooooooh!"

"Haaaaaaaa*raaaaagh!*"

We screamed as we each attempted to overpower the other.

"Whuh...?!"

I won our contest of strength and sent him flying into a trap.

"Second Style—Hazy Moon."

"Huh?!"

A slash attack I had prepared beforehand sliced Raine in the side, throwing him off balance.

"Dark Shadow!"

I attacked again without a moment's delay by sending ten javelins of darkness at him. They looked like a monster opening its large mouth to swallow Raine whole.

"Grr... Guardian Drop!" He quickly surrounded himself with a sphere of water to defend himself, but... "Impossible!"

...the blackness stabbed into the sphere and began to slowly break through.

This defies all reason... How can simple darkness house such ridiculous power?! Raine thought. He quickly dispelled Guardian Drop and jumped back in retreat.

"*Haah, haah*... I seem to be at a disadvantage in close combat...," Raine observed calmly, his shoulders heaving. He sighed heavily and brough his sword aloft.

...*This is gonna be a big one,* I thought. He was focusing a massive amount of spirit power into his tachi, readying a powerful attack.

"I recommend you don't dodge this move. You'll regret it if you do," Raine warned, flicking his eyes to the unconscious senior holy knights behind me.

"You're right..."

If I evaded this move, it would be bad news for the senior holy knights. Blocking it was my only option.

"To think I'd have to play dirty while facing a child...," Raine muttered inaudibly before sheathing his tachi. "...Prepare yourself."

"Bring it on!"

The air tensed as Raine drew his blade with determination.

"Take this—Dragon Drop!"

Raine sent an enormous dragon made of water rushing at me.

"H-how much spirit power is that?!" Lia gasped.

"Dodge it, Allen!" Rose shouted.

The girls were both shocked by the size of the attack.

...*This is an insane amount of spirit power.* A direct hit from this technique would likely kill me. I waited until the water dragon was right in front of me and unleashed my strongest close-range attack.

"Fifth Style—World Render!"

I opened up a fissure in the world with my sword, cleaving the water dragon in two. Enormous shockwaves blasted away the ceiling and walls of the castle, exposing us to the gentle rain. Raine and I met eyes.

"...You blocked Dragon Drop. I'm impressed, Allen. You have done well to obtain such strength at such a young age. I can tell from your exceptional god-given talent, your small yet tempered body, and your honed swordcraft that you've overcome hellish training. You have my respect," Raine said with a smile. "With continued growth, you would surely become one of the greatest swordsmen in the world. That's what makes this so unfortunate. If only I did not have to send you to an early grave."

He gently bit his thumb and used the blood to draw a cross on his chest.

"Forbidden Art—Bloody Robe."

Crimson liquid enveloped Raine's entire body.

"...What did you do?" I asked.

"This is Bloody Robe, a forbidden art that grants me vast power in exchange for shortening my lifespan," Raine answered.

"How formidable."

I maintained the middle stance and stared fixedly at Raine and his Bloody Robe. *I've seen similar techniques before.* His Bloody Robe resembled Lia's Fafnir Soul and Idora's Flying Thunder. They were all techniques that would increase physical strength and amplify the power of your Soul Attire.

"From this point on, this is no longer a simple battle of swordcraft. It's a bloody duel to the death," Raine declared.

"I wouldn't have it any other way," I responded.

Bouts between swordsmen were deadly serious. I didn't want either of us to go easy on the other.

"Hm. Let's do this!"

Raine grinned, and his large body whooshed away from the center of my vision.

"I'm over here," he taunted.

"Yeah, I see you," I responded.

I was able to keep track of him as he zipped behind me, and I ducked to avoid his slash.

"We're just getting started! Guardian Soul Style—Forest Tachi!"

Raine flowed gracefully from a downward slash into a thrust.

I knew he would do that...! It was just the move I'd expected. Raine's swordcraft was fundamental to the core, which made him easy to predict. I flourished my blade to deflect the thrust he was aiming for my stomach.

"Hah!"

"Huh?!"

My perfectly timed counterattack knocked his arms upward, leaving his body wide open. I took advantage by kicking him as hard as I could.

"Yah!"

"Ngh?!"

Raine twisted to avoid a direct hit, and my foot landed hard on his side.

"Gah..."

My blow sent his large, two-meter body soaring through the air. *That felt good. Now's the time to strike!* I shifted my weight to my toes to give chase, but was met with a surprise.

"Not so fast!"

Just then, Raine launched a counterattack, not thrown in the slightest by the pain. That caught me off guard, slowing my reaction by a split second and allowing him to pierce me with a thrust of his tachi.

"Take that!"

"..."

I felt a sharp pain in my left shoulder and jumped back in retreat.

What just happened? I knew I'd kicked him hard. *I thought it would take him a moment to recompose himself. I definitely didn't expect him to counter so quickly...*

I healed my wounded left shoulder with darkness and inspected Raine's body closely. That was when I noticed something—his water cloak had thickened over the spot on his side where I'd kicked him.

"...So it can do that as well," I said. It looked like Raine had used the water surrounding his body to significantly blunt the impact of my attack. The Thirteen Oracle Knights truly were an elite group of swordsmen; he was putting his Soul Attire's power to perfect use. "Your water cloak enhances your offense and defense at the same time. That's really useful."

"Ha. It's not as almighty as your darkness, I'm afraid," Raine responded.

After that exchange, our fight reached a new level of ferocity.

"Haaaaaaaaaa!"

"Ooooooooooh!"

Our swords sent sparks flying as they collided again and again in the rain.

"A-amazing..."

"They're so fast, I can barely keep track of them..."

Lia and Rose watched in blank amazement.

"Cherry Blossom Blade Secret Technique—Mirror Sakura Slash!"

"Guardian Soul Secret Technique—Circle Tachi!"

My eight slashes collided violently with his circular slash, our attacks wiping each other out. We were evenly matched in strength at the moment. *His Bloody Robe is giving me a lot of trouble...* The ability had increased his arm strength, leg strength, and agility significantly.

Something's been different about him, though... Raine's fighting style had become entirely physical since he summoned the Bloody Robe. He had stopped using special moves like Thousand Drop, Colossal Doors, or Mimic Drop entirely. He should have had a number of options at his disposal to give himself the advantage, including raining water arrows on me as he attacked, restraining me with the water hands, or using his copies to overwhelm me with numbers. For some reason, however, he showed no sign of using any of these special techniques.

An explanation occurred to me. *What if this isn't by choice? What if he* can't *use them?* Raine had referred to Bloody Robe as a forbidden art that granted him vast power in exchange for shortening his lifespan. *It's a technique so powerful, it consumes his life. It would make sense if it came with another downside, like preventing him from using other moves.*

I spread a thin cloud of gloom around Raine to test my theory.

"Dark Rain!"

The cloud fired small pieces of darkness resembling raindrops at Raine from all directions. Dark Rain wasn't nearly as powerful as Dark Shadow, but it covered much more ground. The technique prioritized quantity over quality.

How will he deal with this? If Raine could still pull off other techniques, he would surely use Guardian Drop to summon a protective sphere of water and easily ward off my attack. If he didn't, that would prove my theory correct.

"Ngh, Guardian Soul Style —Storm Tachi!"

Raine grimaced and swung his sword like a raging storm. Despite his efforts, however, he was unable to block all the swift drops of darkness.

"Grk..."

A single drop struck his right shoulder and another on his left side.

I knew it! It was just as I'd predicted—Raine couldn't use other abilities while cloaked in the Bloody Robe. *This fight is mine!* There was no need to be overly cautious if he didn't have any hidden tricks up his sleeve. All I needed to do was overpower him!

"Haaaaaaraaaagh!"

I poured a massive amount of spirit power into Zeon, deciding that my next move could win me the fight. Sinister darkness flooded out of my body to form a giant pillar that extended up into the sky.

"How is he so strong...?" Raine asked while looking up at the sky.

"Let's settle this already, Raine!" I shouted.

"Ha, bring it on!" he responded.

Our eyes met before we began our final exchange.

"Dark Shadow!"

"Guardian Soul Style—Flame Tachi! Lightning Tachi! Snow Tachi!"

I unleashed every last bit of darkness I had and sent it hurling toward Raine. He clad himself in a robe of crimson water and swung his sword furiously to defend himself.

"Haaaaaaaaaaa!"

"Oooooooooooh!"

The glimmer of our spirit power lit up the battlefield as my pitch-black darkness and his crimson water repeatedly clashed and vanished. This was now a battle of wills, a grimy war of attrition that ate away at our stamina, spirit power, and mental energy. Whoever lasted longer would win. It was as simple as that.

Raine swung his blade with a desperate fervor, matching my strength completely. "I won't yield… For her sake, for the rest of the children, I'll never yield…!"

It sounded like he was fighting for something he was not going to give up. *I'm the same.* If he overpowered me, it would lead to the deaths of Lia, Rose, Ben and the senior holy knights, and also Mireille and all the citizens of Daglio. Their lives all rested on the strength of my blade. I would never give in, no matter how hard I had to struggle.

"Allen!"

"You can do it!"

Lia and Rose's cheers spurred me on.

""*Haaaaaaaaaarrrrrgggghhh!*""

We both screamed, our eyes filled with determination.

There's no way I'm going to lose, not like this! This is all I have! I had no talent with the sword. My one strength, my only quality I could be truly proud of, was the endurance that had gotten me through over a billion years of training. *I may not have the flashiest fighting style, but that's okay.* I was *not* going to allow anyone to best me in a battle of wills! That was *my* thing!

Keep fighting, no matter how much it hurts! Bear the pain and show what you're made of! Pour everything you have into this moment!

I needed to push myself beyond my limit… That was when I would achieve victory!

"I-I won't give in…!" I yelled.

I stoked the spirit power in my body and increased my output of darkness.

"You're a monster…," Raine gasped.

Seeming to conclude he was at a disadvantage in the face of my endless darkness, Raine took a step back to escape the onslaught.

"I won't let you get away!"

I spread the blackness over a wide area, instantly blinding him.

"Grk… Your control of the darkness is astounding. It's terrifyingly versatile…"

"You're finished—Dark Shadow!"

I swung my ebon blade down and sent sharpened masses of darkness racing toward Raine.

"Guardian Soul Super-Secret Technique—Bladebreaker Tachi!"

Raine deflected each and every one with a single swing. He had condensed his crimson cloak of water around his blade, making his tachi impossibly keen. He'd sacrificed his defense to obtain fearsome power.

"Finally, you show that you are still a child! You're naive if you think you can rush your way to victory… Huh?!"

Astonishment painted Raine's face. There was a good reason for that—I was already in striking range.

"You truly are an elite swordsman, Raine. I knew you would be able to deflect Dark Shadow," I said.

Raine Grad was the greatest swordfighter I had ever fought. I was confident he would be able to overcome Dark Shadow. That was why I'd prepared a follow-up attack.

"…Impressive, Allen Rodol," Raine responded. He closed his eyes.

"Seventh Style—Draw Flash!"

My lightning-quick draw slash severed Eternity Drop and slashed him deep in the stomach.

"Blargh..."

Raine swayed and collapsed slowly backward. He would not be able to keep fighting. I had won.

"Hmm-hmm... *cough, cough*... Ha-ha-ha... I never imagined I would lose after exerting so much of my strength... I actually feel refreshed in defeat..."

He breathed heavily as he laughed. His voice sounded at once happy and sad.

"Surrender yourself to the holy knights, Raine," I urged.

"...The victor does normally have the right over life and death, but... As I said before, this is no longer a battle of swordcraft. Forgive me," Raine said remorsefully.

He drew a strange pattern on the floor with his blood. Moments later, the whole castle began to shake, and crimson beams of light rushed out in all directions. The beams converged and rebounded off each other as they weaved what looked like a giant magic circle out of a fairy tale.

"Wh-what is this?!" I exclaimed. I looked beyond the ruined castle and saw the eerie crimson light expanding all the way to the horizon. The magic circle was likely covering all of Daglio. "What did you do, Raine?!"

"I released all of the spirit power I've spent the last few years storing in this land," he responded.

"What?!"

One of the Thirteen Oracle Knights had spent years storing away this spirit power. Releasing all of it at once would cause destruction on the scale of a natural disaster.

"This whole region is about to become a wasteland. You, Fafnir's host, and all of the senior holy knights will die, putting an end to this whole affair."

"D-don't be stupid! That'll kill you, too!"

"No, it will not. It is my spirit power, after all. I will likely be hurt, but I will not die." Raine gazed into the sky with hollow eyes, looking at the thick rain clouds visible through the collapsed roof of the castle. "...You're too strong, Allen. Loath as I am to admit it, I cannot defeat you alone. That is why I have opted to perform a 'reset.'"

I didn't know what he meant by that, but I heard despair in his voice.

"This land is about to be mercilessly destroyed. There will be nothing left... Losing Fafnir is a bit of a shame, but other eidolons have been accounted for. I will have to fulfill the quota another time."

I spoke up as Raine stood there in silence, his eyes closed.

"I'm sorry, but I won't let you reset anything. You're not killing Lia, Rose, or any of the holy knights!"

"Hmph, so you say... Struggle all you wish. Your efforts will be futile. *Crimson Drop,*" Raine muttered. Red raindrops began to trickle from the thick rain clouds.

"...Huh?"

It was at that moment that I understood just how hopeless—how reckless—my claim had been.

"Y-you're kidding..."

The Crimson Drops falling from the sky were destruction incarnate. They contained explosive spirit power on a scale I had never seen. If they hit the ground, it wasn't just the area surrounding the castle that would become a wasteland—it was the entire country of Daglio.

"I can't stop it... It's impossible..."

This was one of the Thirteen Oracle Knights' ultimate attack, one that he'd built up over a period of years. Its strength exceeded the realm of humanity. In dumbfounded silence, I watched the drops fall.

"Conquer—Dragon King Fafnir!"

"Blossom—Winter Sakura!"

I was brought out of my daze when the wounded Lia and Rose stood on either side of me and summoned their Soul Attires.

"It's okay, Allen. You've got us!" Lia said.

"We're here to help!" Rose declared.

They both took a determined step forward.

...*I see.* It seemed like I had misevaluated the situation. *I had to do something... I had to fix this... I had to do my best...* I'd never had any friends growing up, so I had formed a habit of thinking I had to do everything by myself. But I was no longer alone—I had two valuable friends with me now in Lia and Rose.

I wasn't going to do this alone. It was no longer *I*—it was *us.* From here on out, I was going to fight together with my friends.

"...Thank you, Lia and Rose."

I gripped the black sword tightly with newfound resolve.

"Come on, Allen. Don't forget about us, now."

"Ben?! Are you okay?!" I exclaimed.

"Heh, as you can see, we're all beat to hell, but veterans like us can't just sit on our asses while you young folks show such incredible grit! Isn't that right, you guys?!" Ben called out.

"Do you even need to ask?!"

"Let's show the pride of senior holy knights!"

"W-we've still got plenty of fight left!"

The senior holy knights shouted in response as they climbed to their feet.

"That's what I wanna see!" Ben said, nodding satisfactorily. "We may not be much help, but give us our chance to shine, too!"

"Thank you, that's very reassuring!" I responded.

Now filled with courage and strength, I lifted my head again to face the destructive Crimson Drops.

"You can do it, mister!"

When I did so, I heard a familiar child's voice from behind me.

"Mireille?!"

I turned around to see Mireille holding a tiny shovel. The rest of the citizens of Lao Village were behind her holding hoes, plows, and other types of farm equipment that could be used as weapons.

"Young Allen, please help Lao Village. Please save Daglio," the mayor pleaded. He bowed to me, and the other villagers followed suit.

"Leave it to me!" I said.

Our morale now as high as could be, Ben raised his voice. "It's time for the final gambit! Clean out those ears and listen up! Our targets are the giant red drops falling from the sky! The plan couldn't be simpler—use your best long-range attacks to wipe them the hell out!"

""""Yes, sir!""""

Ben clapped me on the shoulders after he'd finished giving out orders. "We're gonna give everything we have to shrink those drops down even a little. The final blow will be up to you."

"You got it!" I responded.

"All right, everyone! Unleash your full spirit power!"

""""Yes, sir!""""

Ben and the others summoned their Soul Attires and faced the Crimson Drops.

"Blast Seed!"

"Supreme Dragon Breath!"

"Sakura Blizzard!"

The sky was blanketed by a great number of long-range attacks, including Ben's seed bombs, Lia's flames, and Rose's cherry blossom petals. They maintained their all-out attacks for a little less than a minute before one by one they began to run out of spirit power and buckle over from exhaustion.

"Haah, haah... Sorry, Allen... I'm all out of spirit power...," Ben panted.

"Take care of the rest, Allen...," Lia urged.

"I wanted to shrink them more, but... I've hit my limit...," Rose admitted.

They breathlessly passed the baton to me.

"Thanks, guys," I responded.

They had done enough. I knew I could manage with the strength they had given me.

"Phew..."

I looked up to see the sky covered by the Crimson Drops. They roared as they fell and could easily have been mistaken for meteorites. *They're huge...* I was sure everyone's all-out attacks had chipped them down in size, but now that they were closer to the ground, they seemed even larger than before.

"...This is a lot of pressure."

All of Daglio would be wiped out if those drops hit the earth. That would almost certainly mean our deaths as well. I gripped the black sword tightly, closed my eyes, and concentrated.

...I don't have full command over Zeon's power yet. I had, however, crossed blades many times with the best sparring partner I could ask for.

Remember his *darkness.* Thick gloom so complete, it made one recoil in fear. *Picture that power in my hands.* I needed full control over that indomitable strength. *Imagine the mightiest version of me...and project it here and now!*

I poured every last bit of the spirit power I had left into Zeon, and a whole new level of darkness erupted out of me. Black as an abyss, it crept across the earth as if it had a mind of its own, dyeing the crimson magic circle black and covering the entirety of Daglio in seconds flat.

"""""
...

Silence reigned as the bizarre sight caused everyone's breath to catch in their throats.

This is my full power! Holding the black and heavy sword of the abyss, I performed my strongest long-range attack.

"Sixth Style—Dark Boom!"

The ultimate black slash attack flew up into the sky to slam into the Crimson Drops. An enormous shockwave traveled the earth, and I heard screams everywhere.

Th-they're so heavy... A greater shock than I had ever felt raced up my arms, and intense wind assaulted my cheeks. *Crap...they're going to overpower me at this rate...*

An Oracle Knight had spent years building up this move. It contained a colossal amount of spirit power, and the kinetic energy from their fall gave the drops unimaginable destructive force.

"It's no use, Allen! Crimson Drop is going to destroy everything. You can't stop it, no matter how strong you are! It will never stop raining in Daglio! I can't let you ruin this...!" Raine yelled, his voice full of emotion.

""""LET'S GO, ALLEN!"""""

Ben and the holy knights drowned out Raine's voice with deep cheers of encouragement.

"Keep fighting, mister!"

"I know you can do it, Allen! I believe in you!"

"Please, Allen... Don't give up...!"

Mireille's ear-splitting yell, Rose's inspiring words, and finally, Lia's heartfelt plea filled me with strength.

Everyone's hopes and lives are resting on this blade. There's no way I'm going to lose... I'd spent over one billion years tirelessly polishing my swordcraft. *I'm going to use this strength to protect everyone!*

I found a firm, unwavering resolve. At that moment, a strange blackness surged out of my body. *What is this...?!* It was different from the cold, wicked darkness I had used up to this point. It was warm and kind, and felt somehow nostalgic.

The new kind of darkness joined its counterpart as it enveloped Dark Boom, significantly powering it up enough to allow it to start forcing back the Crimson Drops.

This is gonna work!

Seeing my first and only chance of victory, I screamed from the bottom of my lungs.

"CLEAR UUUUUUUUUP!"

Immense black swallowed the red, instantly wiping the destructive Crimson Drops out of existence. The thick clouds that covered the sky parted to reveal bright and gentle sunlight.

"I-I did it…," I muttered.

""""YEEAAAAAHHHHH!""""

Cheers exploded throughout Daglio.

"That was the most amazing thing I've ever seen, Allen!" Lia exclaimed, jumping into my chest.

"You really are amazing…!" Rose said, patting me on the shoulders.

Ben and the other senior holy knights rushed toward me next.

"Great job, Allen!"

"I can't believe how much spirit power you packed into that black slash attack!"

"You're not human!"

"That was glorious! You're now Allen Rodol, the Savior of Daglio!"

The holy knights mobbed me in their excitement, looking like they wanted to party the rest of the day.

We continued to bask in our victory over Raine Grad until, once again, it started to rain. The rain was nothing compared to before, though—it was so gentle, it could hardly even be considered a drizzle. I looked up and saw a thin rain cloud hanging over the castle.

"*Haah, haah…*"

I turned around to look at Raine. Despite his heavy injuries, he was groveling on the ground and gripping his broken Soul Attire, looking half-dead as he desperately used what little spirit power he had left to make it rain.

What is possibly driving Raine to fight this hard? I wondered.

"Hey, quit your pointless resistance!" one of the senior holy knights shouted, raising his sheathed sword.

"Stop!"

Just then, a girl no more than nine years old jumped in front of Raine to protect him.

"Wh-who are you...? Where did you come from?" the senior holy knight asked in confusion.

"S-Serena?! Why did you come out here?!" Raine asked, widening his eyes and shaking her shoulders.

"I-I had to... They were bullying you, Father...," Serena answered.

"I see... You truly are a kind girl..."

I looked around as I listened to them and saw that a part of the floor had been lifted up. *A hidden door.* Upon closer observation, it was covered in a thin layer of water; Raine must have put it there as a defensive measure against Eternity Drop before hiding her there. The fact he was making it rain likely had something to do with her as well.

"Hey, Raine, do you want to talk? I get the sense you were forced into this somehow," I said.

Why would a man who called the Black Organization "scum" join their ranks? Why was he so insistent on making it rain? And who was Serena? I felt like that last question was the most important of all. *I just can't see Raine as being a bad person deep down.* He must have had a major reason to do what he'd done.

"..."

Raine gritted his teeth and looked around, eventually settling his eyes on Serena. He was probably trying to decide what course of action would be in her best interest.

"We're taking you back to the Holy Knights Association. You should tell us the whole story if you care about this girl," I urged.

Would Raine tell the truth, or would he remain silent? That choice would have a huge impact on the severely his crimes were judged, and how Serena would be treated. Raine had to know that.

"...Very well," he acquiesced after a long silence. "I once founded an orphanage in a small war-torn nation. I gathered children who had been robbed of their families, and we all helped one another survive. We were dirt-poor, yet our days were full of happiness..."

Raine sounded as if he was reflecting on the good old days.

"It took just one night for all our happiness to collapse... It started like any other peaceful spring day. I still remember every detail. We tilled the fields and ate lunch together as we always did, and then I left for my monthly shopping trip. I bought the bare necessities at a distant black market...and returned to a sight out of hell. All of my beloved children...had been eaten by monsters..."

He clenched his fists, and his voice trembled as he thought back to that moment.

"I immediately drew my sword and slaughtered the offending creatures. As I stood in that sea of blood, I was overwhelmed by helplessness, a sense of loss I knew I would never overcome, and an intense despair... What I felt in that moment cannot be put into words. I was completely sapped of the will to live. Then, just when I thought that I needed to perform a burial for everyone, one girl came back to life. It was Serena."

Raine gave her a loving embrace.

"I rushed her to the hospital and spent everything I had to my name getting her treated. The doctors were able to save her life, but...it turned out the monsters had given her the worst parting gift imaginable—a curse."

Curses were an unexplained power some monsters possessed. Almost nothing was known about their effects, what triggered them, or how to dispel them.

"Serena was inflicted with a Rain Curse. Those affected won't be harmed wherever it is raining, but their bodies will sear with scorching pain the moment they step away from the rain. Eventually, it kills you. My heart sank when the doctors told me. The curse had a one hundred percent mortality rate..."

Her death had been guaranteed.

"After that, I zipped back and forth across the continent with Serena, desperately seeking places where it was raining by relying on newspaper weather forecasts. That was never going to last, though.

The rain clouds disappeared once summer arrived. I could only look on as the blazing sun tortured poor Serena... I wailed, cursing my powerlessness and the cruelty of fate—and then God appeared before me."

"...God?"

"Yes. A mysterious old man who called himself the Time Hermit."

"..."

My breath caught in my throat. I hadn't expected to hear that name. *The Time Hermit?! Is Raine also a Transcendent who broke free of the 100-Million-Year Button's curse?!* I slowly exhaled to calm myself and listened to Raine's continuation.

"God used his power to invite me to a strange world. My time there was hellish. I spent years enduring terrible loneliness and intense training, but at the end of it all, I finally obtained a Soul Attire called Eternity Drop, which has the ability to produce rain."

Raine glanced at his broken tachi.

"I trembled with joy. I could use this power to render the curse harmless. Serena could live a normal life. But that happiness was short-lived. We were driven out of the village in less than a month."

Raine continued on, his expression haggard.

"The rain can only be summoned around the caster. It follows me wherever I go. And I couldn't hide the fact that I was the source of the rain for very long. 'Get lost, Rainbringer,' they shouted as they kicked us out."

If he could only make it rain around himself, it would only be a matter of time before he was found out.

"I moved to a different village with Serena after that, but the rumor of the Rainbringer spread quickly, and we were kicked out yet again. We spent some time wandering aimlessly until I received an invitation from the Black Organization. They wanted me to join them."

Oh yeah... Chairwoman Reia said that the Black Organization was gathering Transcendents. They must have learned that he had pushed the 100-Million-Year Button through the work of their independent information network.

"I refused at first, of course...but they must have expected that, for they offered me a deal."

"...A deal?"

"Yes. It seemed they had done thorough research on us... They told me this: 'Capture a monster known as an eidolon, and we will give you an entire country. You can live with Serena there and make it rain all you want.'"

The organization had offered him a deal knowing all about the Rain Curse and their dire situation.

"It didn't take long for me to make my decision. It is impossible for one person to conquer an entire nation, but with the backing of the Black Organization—and by extension, the powerful Holy Ronelian Empire—it was trivial. So I sold my soul to the Devil. I am fully aware I have done wrong. But I swore something to myself at that time—that I would honor the children who died by making Serena happy."

I saw resolve burning in Raine's eyes.

"You know the rest. I turned Daglio from the Land of Sunshine into the Land of Rain... And that's all I can tell you."

The sympathy and pity everyone was feeling for Raine and Serena was palpable. I broke the silence with a proposal.

"I might be able to do something about that Rain Curse."

"...What?" Raine said.

"My darkness can heal anything other than illnesses. That includes monster hexes."

"D-don't lie to me! There is zero precedent for healing a curse! Not even a rare healing Soul Attire would be able to do anything!"

"That may be the case, but...I'm certain that I can heal it."

How could I get him to believe me? As I thought about that, Raine gulped and looked at me straight in the eyes.

"Can you truly...help Serena?" he asked.

"Yes. There's no doubt in my mind I can," I answered.

"Huh…" He dragged himself to his feet despite his injuries and bowed deeply. "I know I shame myself by asking this after all I have done… But please, I beg of you—can you remove Serena's curse?"

"Yes, of course."

I readily agreed to Raine's request and took a look at Serena's curse.

"It's this weird bruise," the girl said, opening her right hand. There was a dark red pattern on her palm.

It looks a lot like Ries's curse. It looked like I would be able to heal it without issue.

"Okay, please hold still," I said.

"O-okay…," she responded.

I wrapped darkness around Serena's right palm. I made the darkness thin and gentle, and focused on removing the invasive presence. Her dark red skin quickly returned to its normal, clear color.

"I-it's gone…?" Serena said.

"Did you actually do it?!" Raine gasped.

They both looked as if they had just witnessed pure magic.

"All right, you should be fine now. Raine, can you please stop the rain?" I asked.

"S-sure…!" He cut off his spirit power, and the light drizzle stopped.

"Serena, how do you feel?" I inquired.

"I feel great! Thank you, sir!" Serena responded, beaming with joy.

"You're welco—" I began with a kind smile, but I got interrupted when Raine grasped my hand with tears streaking down his face. "R-Raine…"

"Thank you. Thank you so much, Allen…! I will never forget the debt of gratitude I owe you. I promise I'll return the favor someday…," he said, thanking me repeatedly.

The senior holy knights took Raine and Serena away shortly afterward. I was worried about what was going to happen to them, so I asked Ben for his thoughts on the matter.

"There's no need to worry about Serena. She hasn't committed any

crime, and she's still a minor. I'm sure she'll live a normal life at an
orphanage managed by the Holy Knights Association. As for Raine…
I'm not so sure."

He crossed his arms and groaned.

"He's one of the Thirteen Oracle Knights, a member of the enemy's
top brass… I'm too low on the chain to have any guess at what kind of
punishment the higher-ups will decide on for him. I'm confident of one
thing, though—they won't give him the death penalty."

"A-are you sure?!"

"Yeah. Raine isn't an evil person at his core, and more importantly
than that, he's strong enough to conquer an entire country. I wouldn't
be surprised if extra-legal measures are taken to lighten his sentence."

"I see…," I said with relief. Just then, a white signal flare shot into
the sky from the direction of the temporary Daglio holy knight branch.
"What is that?"

"One white flare means a message from headquarters. The higher-
ups must have seen the situation here with some kind of remote-viewing
Soul Attire, those lechers," Ben spat, his brow furrowed. Judging by that
reaction, he didn't seem to totally trust upper management. "Sorry,
Allen. Looks like I need to hurry back to the branch and give a detailed
report. I wanted to throw the wildest party you've ever seen to celebrate
what you accomplished, but we'll have to save that for another night."

He apologized guiltily and took off sprinting for the branch.

"I'd rather have a normal celebration party…," I said, but that wish
went unheard.

"Let's go back to the branch, too, Allen," Lia said.

"I second that. Today really wore me out. Let's go relax with everyone," Rose agreed.

"Yeah, we should get going," I responded.

Later, I dazed at the sky absentmindedly as the three of us headed
back to the temporary Daglio branch. *We really went through a lot
here…* We'd freed Daglio from the rule of the Black Organization,

stopped the endless rain, and healed the curse that had caused Raine and Serena to suffer. All of those major events had happened in just the last few hours. This truly had been a turbulent day.

I'm glad everything was resolved nicely in the end.

Bright sunlight illuminated Daglio, and the sky was blue as far as the eye could see. The nightmarish rain had finally ended. The Land of Sunshine would once again live up to its nickname.

■

We departed Daglio a few days later while being seen off by Ben and a large crowd of senior holy knights. After a bumpy two-hour flight in a small aircraft, we arrived at the Aurest branch of the Holy Knights Association.

"Phew… Feels like forever since we've been here," I said.

"Yeah, really," Lia agreed.

"We had a really rough time over there…" Rose responded.

We had been in Daglio for only a week, but so much happened in that short amount of time that the air in Liengard actually felt nostalgic.

"Okay… We should go see Mr. Clown first," I said.

"Yeah, we need an explanation," Lia seconded.

"You bet we do," Rose said.

We needed to talk to Clown about our trip to Daglio. He had told us it was a relatively peaceful country and perfect for our first foreign expedition, but that was clearly a lie. Daglio was a war-torn land under the direct control of the Black Organization, and he'd sent us there one day before the showdown with Raine Grad. There was no way he wouldn't have known about that as the manager of the holy knights' Aurest branch.

I'm sure he had his reasons for sending us, but… We needed to get him to explain himself.

Disembarking from the small plane, we headed for the branch manager's office.

■

We passed through reception and straightened our appearances in front of the branch manager's office. Then I cleared my throat and knocked on the door.

"Come in," Clown said casually.

"Excuse us," I said, and stepping inside.

"Hey, guys! Great work down there!" Clown greeted us with a gentle smile on his face.

"Oh my, if it isnae Allen! I'm glad to see you're well."

There was one other person in the room—Rize Dorhein, the manager of Fox Financing.

"Huh? Ms. Rize?" I responded.

"Rize Dorhein…?!" Lia shouted.

"Why is the Blood Fox here…?" Rose asked.

Lia and Rose were shocked by her surprise presence.

"Hee-hee, I heard that ye performed splendidly in Daglio, Allen. I knew I was right tae set my eye on you," Rize said. She giggled with a kind expression on her face. Apparently, she had already heard about the events of the last week.

"Thank you… Why are you here, by the way?" I asked. One of the Five Business Oligarchs shouldn't have much to do with the Aurest branch of the Holy Knights Association.

"Clown is an old friend of mine. I like tae visit him on occasion," Rize responded.

"Ah-ha-ha, I owe Rize a lot," Clown said.

"Huh, I didn't know that."

It was a small world. People were often connected in ways you didn't expect.

I decided to bring up the purpose for our visit after we'd finished our simple greetings.

"By the way, Mr. Clown. We would like to speak to you, if that's okay."

"Y-yeah… I figured you would say that…" He scratched his cheek with an awkward smile. It looked like he had been aware of the situation in Daglio after all. "I am so sorry for doing that to you guys." Clown removed his hat and bowed deeply. There was no hint of his usual facetious manner; the apology appeared as genuine as could be.

"Wow, you sure got serious quick…," Lia said.

"Were there some circumstances that forced your hand?" Rose asked.

The girls were both caught off guard by his genuine expression of regret.

"It's as you said, Rose. I had complicated reasons for sending you to Daglio. This may sound like nothing more than excuses, but will you listen to what I have to say?" Clown asked.

"Yes, of course," I responded. The other two nodded in agreement.

"All right—allow me to start at the end. The reason I sent you three to Daglio the day before the decisive operation was to save Ben and the other senior holy knights stationed at the temporary branch."

"To save them?"

"Yes. The Holy Knights Association's headquarters underestimated Raine Grad. He is frightfully strong. Ben and the others are certainly skilled fighters…but they're no match for one of the Thirteen Oracle Knights. If HQ had been serious about defeating Raine, they should have sent the Seven Holy Blades."

The Seven Holy Blades was a name given to a group of holy knights who were regarded as the strongest swordfighters in the world.

"Keep this between us, but Ben and I were classmates… I just couldn't let him die. I submitted multiple written opinions to senior management after the date of Operation Annihilation was decided, telling them we were at a clear disadvantage in fighting strength. Those are hardheaded folks, though, and they rejected my every proposal."

Clown scratched his cheek and gave a self-deprecating smile.

"I continued to protest until they got fed up and demoted me just the other week. They kicked me out of headquarters and sent me here. I fretted over what I could do, having lost what little status and authority I had. That's when I received what felt like a blessing from heaven from Thousand Blade Academy."

"From Thousand Blade? Do you mean…"

"Yes. Chairwoman Reia recommended you three as senior holy knight special trainees."

Clown pulled three sheets of paper out of his desk. They were letters of recommendation with our profiles and the Thousand Blade seal.

"As soon as I saw your name, I knew this was a once-in-a-lifetime opportunity, Allen," Clown said with a smile. "To be honest, I have known about you for some time. Rize told me she found an incredible talent, and I don't take an endorsement like that from her lightly."

I glanced at Rize, and she grinned and waved.

"After lucking into such a powerful trump card, I took advantage of it by sending you three to Daglio without informing you of the situation there. But you defeated Shido Jukurius at the Elite Five Holy Festival, Idora Luksmaria at the Sword Master Festival, and captured Rize's heart. Given all that, I was confident you could defeat Raine Grad."

Clown's expression was as serious as could be.

"And my gamble paid off. Operation Annihilation succeeded without a single casualty among the senior holy knights, and it was all thanks to you, Allen. You beat back the Black Organization in Lao Village and healed all the villagers, defeated Raine, and destroyed the Crimson Drops. I've heard you did everything and more. You have my sincere thanks for saving Ben and the others."

Clown thanked me profusely and bowed once again.

"That said, none of that changes the fact that I deceived you three. I am truly sorry for what I put you through."

His apology appeared as earnest as could be.

"...I understand why you did it," I said.

Clown made it very clear that he'd tried everything he could to save his old classmate. *We certainly had a rough time, but...* In the end, Lia and Rose were unhurt, and we'd freed Daglio from the Black Organization. Clown had his reasons for tricking us, and he offered us a sincere apology. I personally didn't think there was any more reason to be angry with him.

I looked at Lia and Rose, and they nodded. It seemed like we were all thinking the same thing.

"Mr. Clown, let's sweep all of this under the rug. One thing, though... If a similar situation arises in the future, can you please fill us in on everything first? I would be happy to help anytime."

"...Thank you very much," Clown responded, bowing his head deeply. "Allen, can I ask you for one last favor?" He timidly lifted his index finger.

"A favor?" I repeated.

"That's right. I would rather you not tell anyone about your expedition to Daglio. Including Chairwoman Reia."

"...Why?"

"How should I put this? ...It would be very bad for the Holy Knights Association if this were to become public."

"Huh...? Oh, I see what you mean..."

He was probably concerned about the survival of the Special Trainee Program. That system was just established this year to recruit outstanding students. If word got out that they'd sent special trainees into a war zone, that would greatly decrease the number of applicants. It could lead to the disbandment of the program and, in the worst-case scenario, could put students off on becoming holy knights. That could be the source of Clown's anxieties.

"I know I am in no position to ask this, but...for the sake of the growth of the Holy Knights Association—and by extension, the safety of the world—can you please keep quiet about what happened in Daglio?" Clown asked, bowing again in entreaty.

On the off chance that word of this incident did cause students to lose interest in becoming holy knights, the Holy Knights Association would decline, and the world would become even more unstable. I obviously didn't want that to happen...and besides, it was really difficult to refuse such a fervent request.

I guess there wouldn't be much of a problem with us staying quiet about what happened in Daglio... This incident was an anomaly; I highly doubted something like it would happen again.

"*Haah...* Fine. We won't tell anyone about what happened in Daglio," I consented after giving in.

"I knew you would understand, Allen! You're a lifesaver!" Clown exclaimed, returning to his usual casual demeanor... There was definitely something fishy about him. "All right! Allen promised to keep his lips sealed, so can I expect the same from you two, Lia and Rose...?" Clown asked, rubbing his hands together.

"Geez, you're way too nice, Allen...," Lia said.

"I'm with Lia on this one...," Rose added.

They sighed together and promised not to breathe a word about what happened in Daglio.

Having finished our discussion with Clown, we left the branch manager's office and returned to our Thousand Blade dorms for the first time in a week.

■

Allen, Lia, and Rose had left the branch manager's office.

"Phew... Wasn't sure we'd be able to pull that off," Clown said with relief.

"Allen truly is a nice boy... It takes a lot tae make him angry," Rize responded.

"He's just like they say he is—straight as an arrow and way too nice for his own good…"

Clown began to plot about how he could use the boy. Allen had shown himself to be capable of anything.

"Clown? Just a warning… Ye do know what I'll do if you take advantage of his kindness for yer own schemes, right?" Rize warned with a gentle smile. She'd seen right through him.

A threatening, suffocating aura filled the room.

Th-that's not a warning, that's an outright threat…, Clown thought.

Rize was even more attached to Allen Rodol than he'd thought. Realizing that, he immediately abandoned the schemes involving Allen he had dreamt up and shook his head exaggeratedly.

"All right, all right! I won't mess with your golden child again!"

"Glad tae hear it."

The malice in the room dissipated, and Clown sighed softly.

Haah… It's a heck of a waste, but it looks like it would be in my best interest to stay away from Allen… Clown had known Rize for long enough to know how merciless, possessive, and persistent she was. *There's something…weird about her attachment to him, though…*

Rize was a fickle person, for better or worse. Something she prized one day could become trash in her eyes the next. The one thing she truly treasured was her little sister, Ferris Dorhein. It was unusual for her to remain fixated on a single individual for months at a time.

She's still hiding something… There must have been more to Allen Rodol than Clown was privy to. Feeling sure of that, he decided he would perform a private investigation into Allen while taking care not to incur Rize's wrath.

"Allen has become such a dependable young man… He is almost unrecognizable from the time I met him at the Unity Festival. *Haah,* if only I was a wee bit younger…," Rize sighed.

"Yeah, can't say you have much chance over thirty—" Clown was interrupted when his hat withered like a flower and vanished.

"I'm still twenty-nine. Don't *ever* make that mistake again," Rize warned, her northern accent completely gone. That happened only when she was truly furious.

"I-I'm sorry...," Crown apologized sincerely, fearing for his life. He quickly searched for another topic. "O-oh yeah, Allen has finally realized his Soul Attire! Does this mean the Black Organization is going to start pursuing him in earnest?"

"Hmm, I wonder... Allen has defeated two of the Thirteen Oracle Knights—Fuu Ludoras and Raine Grad—in the last couple months. I wouldnae be surprised if they sent an assassin after him...," Rize responded as if she had no stake in the matter.

"Aren't you gonna interfere? One of the top Oracle Knights could decide to go after him next."

"Hee-hee, that boy willnae go down so easily. How could he, with Zeon as his Spirit Core!" Rize's eyes sparkled like a little girl's. "Can ye even imagine it, Clown? He's already taken Zeon's power at fifteen years old."

"He's insanely talented...," Clown agreed, continuing with a conflicted smile. "I kinda feel for him, though."

"What do ye mean?"

"He's just carrying a really heavy burden... Honestly, I'd abandon everything and run if I were him!"

"Hee-hee, his mental fortitude is nae longer human... He probably spent an unthinkable amount of time in the World of Time. Perhaps even...the full one hundred million years?" Rize said jokingly, and Clown burst out laughing.

"Now, that I don't find very likely. The longest stint in the World of Time on record is one thousand years," Clown responded.

"Hmm-hmm, ye're right. It was just a joke."

They both laughed at how absurd that was, but the reality was even harder to believe. Allen had actually gone through more than ten loops of the hellish World of Time, spending over one billion years there.

"I need tae get back to Drestia. I have a business meeting," Rize said.

"Got it! I'll make sure Ben and the others keep quiet, just as we agreed before," Clown responded.

"Make it quick, okay? If ye take too long, they'll give Allen away."

Rize wanted to erase all traces of Allen Rodol's involvement in the Daglio incident. She had one reason for that—to conceal his existence.

Hmm-hmm, he's going tae get so much stronger!

Rize had been waiting for Allen to reach his full, unrivaled potential. Biding her time for the revolution he was going to bring about in the world.

Hee-hee, I cannae wait...

And so the secret conversation between Rize Dorhein and Clown Jester—two people whose schemes had taken root in society's underbelly—came to an end.

■

After returning from Daglio, I spent the entirety of the small amount of time left of our break on practice swings. December 1 marked our return to classes.

Lia and I walked to campus and greeted everyone when we entered Class 1-A. Our peers looked a little tougher. We naturally had plenty to talk about because we hadn't seen one another in a week, and before I knew it, the bell announcing the start of homeroom rang. We took our seats right as Chairwoman Reia burst through the door.

"Good morning, boys and girls! I'm sure you all made good use of your long break! Now's the time when I would normally move us right into first period, but... Rejoice! One of the most exciting things that can happen at school is taking place today—we're getting a transfer student!" she declared loudly, and everyone began talking at once.

"Wow, a transfer student...I wonder what kind of person they are?!"

"Are they a boy or a girl?!"

"They must be really skilled if they're transferring to an Elite Five Academy."

"Mwa-ha-ha, rejoice, you rascals! The transfer student is a drop-dead gorgeous swordswoman! Come on in!" the chairwoman called.

The door to the classroom swung open, and in walked someone I knew all too well.

You've got to be kidding me...

She was about 165 centimeters tall and had black, glossy hair that reached her shoulders. Her facial features were elegant and beautiful, her skin smooth and white, and her figure slender. The gracefulness of her appearance drew eyes even from a distance. And though unusual for a girl, she wore the male Thousand Blade uniform.

It was the captain of the Vesteria Royal Guard—Claude. She walked gracefully to the podium and cleared her throat.

"I am Claude Stroganof from Royal Vesteria Academy. Nice to meet you," she said.

"C-Claude?!" Lia shouted, jumping up from her seat with shock on her face.

"Long time no see, Your Highness!" Claude smiled gently at Lia. "And...I see you're still alive and kicking, maggot," she said, glaring openly at me.

"Ah-ha-ha... It's been a while, Claude...," I responded. I was disappointed that she was back to calling me "maggot," but I decided to let it slide for now. *Haah... I smell more trouble in my future...*

I sighed loudly, thinking about the implications of Claude's transfer. My stomach hurt.

Afterword

Thank you very much to everyone who picked up the fifth volume of *100-Million-Year Button*! I am the author, Syuichi Tsukishima.

I would like to start by briefly touching on the content of this novel. This will contain spoilers, so please be careful if you are the type to read the afterword first.

Volume 5 is composed of two parts: the White Lily Girls Academy arc, and the Daglio arc. The White Lily section features fierce fights, along with appearances from Idora, Shido, and Cain! The story turned out to be lively and fun. By contrast, the Daglio section is one violent battle after another! The fight against Raine is the most intense yet!

I think splitting Volume 5 into two parts made for a focused novel. I'll be happy if it brings even a little joy to my readers.

Volume 6 will contain the Christmas arc, the demon arc, and more. It's shaping up to be jam-packed! (I am currently working on the manuscript!) The Japanese release date is scheduled for four months from now, on February 20 of next year!

Furthermore, the long-awaited first volume of *100-Million-Year Button*'s manga version will be released in Japan in ten days, on October 26! You can see Allen, Lia, and Rose in manga form! I am taking part in the production as well, and the end of the volume features three special short stories starring Allen, Lia, and Rose! Please check that out as well!

Now I'd like to give some words of thanks. To the illustrator, Mokyu, to the lead editor, the proofreader, and everyone else who worked on this book—thank you very much.

May we meet again in Volume 6 in four months on February 20.

Syuichi Tsukishima